The Cutie Mark Chronicles
Volume I

by Penumbra Quill

Little, Brown and Company
New York Boston

My Little Pony: Ponyville Mysteries: Schoolhouse of Secrets originally published in July 2017 by Little, Brown and Company
My Little Pony: Ponyville Mysteries: Tail of the Timberwolf originally published in July 2017 by Little, Brown and Company
My Little Pony: Ponyville Mysteries: Riddle of the Rusty Horseshoe originally published in October 2017 by Little, Brown and Company

Cover design by Christina Quintero. Cover art by Franco Spagnolo.

Little, Brown and Company
Hachette Book Group
1290 Avenue of the Americas, New York, NY 10104
Visit us at LBYR.com

First Bindup Edition: September 2018

Little, Brown and Company is a division of Hachette Book Group, Inc.
The Little, Brown name and logo are trademarks of Hachette Book Group, Inc.

The publisher is not responsible for websites (or their content) that are not owned by the publisher.

ISBNs: 978-0-316-41933-8 (pbk.), 978-0-316-45152-9 (ebook)

Printed in the United States of America

LSC-C

10 9 8 7 6 5 4 3 2 1

CONTENTS

Schoolhouse
of Secrets

The Pony stared out the window at the
quaint cottages spread out below. Ponyville
was small. Much smaller than from where
The Pony had traveled. The large and tacky
castle nearby was clearly a later addition
and, in The Pony's opinion, stuck out
like a sore hoof. But then, the princesses
of Equestria were never known for being
subtle.

However, it was the endless forest
beginning at the very edge of town that
truly held The Pony's attention. This was
why The Pony had uprooted everything
to move to this backcountry village. The
Everfree Forest contained secrets yet to
be discovered. Ancient secrets. Dangerous

secrets. Secrets that would make the pony who uncovered them very powerful. And now, here The Pony was, living just a few short steps away.

It was time to get started.

It was another typically perfect morning in Ponyville. The sun shone brightly as ponies, Unicorns, and Pegasi bustled about. They opened their shops, ran early-morning errands, and generally got their days started. Some of the younger members of Ponyville rushed through town toward the Schoolhouse. Apple Bloom, Sweetie Belle, and Scootaloo trotted alongside one another, just like they did every morning. Apple Bloom usually talked nonstop the entire way to school, but not today. Scootaloo smacked her with a wing.

"Spill it!" she ordered.

"What?" Apple Bloom asked.

"You're really quiet this morning,"

Sweetie Belle explained. "You not talking? That's weird."

"It's nothin'!" Apple Bloom said casually. Snips and Snails rushed past them toward the Schoolhouse.

"Mornin', Crusaders!" Snips called. "Hey, Apple Bloom! Sweetie Belle! Tell your sisters they are *awesome!*"

"We *will!*" Sweetie Belle called back. Apple Bloom sighed. Scootaloo and Sweetie Belle glanced at each other.

"Sister stuff," Scootaloo said. Sweetie Belle nodded in agreement. Scootaloo turned to Apple Bloom. "Okay, what's up?"

Apple Bloom stopped walking and turned toward her best friends. "What are we doin' with our lives?" she asked. Sweetie Belle and Scootaloo stared at her.

"Right now we're going to school," Sweetie Belle responded.

"What do you *think* we should be doing?" Scootaloo asked.

Pip hurried past them, awkwardly dragging a schoolbag that was much too big for him. "Cheerio, ponies! Apple Bloom, Sweetie Belle, tell your sisters top-notch job!"

Apple Bloom gritted her teeth.

"This is about Applejack, Rarity, and that Manticore, isn't it?" Sweetie Belle asked. Apple Bloom nodded. A few days ago, Rarity and Applejack were returning from a friendship mission for Princess Twilight Sparkle when the Friendship Express was attacked by a crazed Manticore. *Of course,* the two of them rushed to the rescue, saved a bunch of ponies, figured out what the misunderstanding was, befriended the creature, and saved the day. It was all *any*pony in Ponyville could talk about.

"What? You wish they *didn't* defeat the Manticore?" Sweetie Belle asked.

"Of course not," Apple Bloom said defensively.

"Are you afraid Applejack is gonna like the Manticore more than you? Invite him to live in your room?" Scootaloo asked, grinning.

"No!" Apple Bloom said, laughing.

"Oooh. I bet the Manticore can buck *so many* more apples than you!" Sweetie Belle giggled. "If I were you I'd be really worried!"

"I'm not worried!" Apple Bloom exclaimed. "I'm just wonderin' what's next for the Cutie Mark Crusaders."

"What do you mean?" Scootaloo asked.

"Well, it just seems like there's gotta be something more out there for us to do." It was the first time Apple Bloom had expressed her concern out loud.

"We've been helping other ponies figure out *their* cutie marks," Sweetie Belle answered. "After all, we've had plenty of experience with that!"

"I know, and don't get me wrong. I love that *our* cutie marks are all about helpin' *other* ponies with their cutie marks." The Crusaders examined their cutie marks. Each of them had a matching shield with a different symbol inside. Apple Bloom had a heart inside an apple, Sweetie Belle had a music note inside a star, and Scootaloo had a lightning bolt inside a wing. They were the only ponies they knew in Equestria to have cutie marks that matched this way. "But don't y'all wish it was a bit more…exciting sometimes?"

"*Exciting* sounds like another word for *dangerous*," Sweetie Belle admitted.

"You know I'm always up for an adventure," Scootaloo said. "But think about it. We didn't get our cutie marks until *after* we stopped looking for them, right? Maybe some big adventure will pop up when we least expect it to!" Apple Bloom considered that as Diamond Tiara and Silver Spoon came trotting up behind them.

"Morning, Crusaders!" Diamond Tiara called in her singsongy voice. "Did you hear—"

"*Yes!*" Apple Bloom yelled. "*We know all about my sister and Rarity and the Manticore!*" Everypony stared at Apple Bloom, who blushed brightly.

"Sorry 'bout that," she muttered.

"What I was *about* to say before I was *interrupted*," continued Diamond Tiara, "was, 'Did you hear about the family that moved into that old house up on Horseshoe Hill?' There's a *new filly* starting school today and nopony knows *anything* about her except *me*!"

CHAPTER TWO

"My mother heard that her whole family moved here from Trotsylvania," Diamond Tiara explained as they approached the Schoolhouse. She hadn't stopped talking about this new family since she had joined the Crusaders on their walk. "My father says they must be pretty well-off to have bought that house. It's *huge!*"

"I wonder why they moved here," Apple Bloom said. It had been a while since anypony new had come to Ponyville.

"Hey! Maybe we should give the new student a nice, warm welcome!" Sweetie Belle suggested. "Show her how nice it is here in Ponyville?"

"That's a *great* idea!" Scootaloo chimed

in. "And who better to welcome her than the Cutie Mark Crusaders! Right, Apple Bloom?"

Apple Bloom grinned. A Cutie Mark Crusaders welcoming committee might not be the same as saving a train full of ponies from a Manticore, but it would certainly make this new student's day better!

"Sure," she agreed. "Let's go meet this new pony and show her what Ponyville has to offer!" The school bell rang and the ponies hurried toward the Schoolhouse.

"Okay, students! Hurry up!" Miss Cheerilee called from the doorway. "We've got a big day planned!"

Apple Bloom rushed up the stairs behind Scootaloo and Sweetie Belle. There was a buzz of activity as everypony bustled around the room, chatting and joking.

Apple Bloom scanned the room but didn't see anypony aside from the ones she already knew. The hustle and bustle of the room suddenly came to a complete stop. Apple Bloom looked around to see why the students were suddenly so quiet. They were all staring in the direction of the door to the Schoolhouse. Apple Bloom followed their gazes and saw the new student, standing quietly and observing them.

She was a lavender-coated Unicorn. Her bright-blue mane had white streaks in it, as did her tail. Her piercing violet eyes glared out at everypony staring back at her. On her flank was her cutie mark, a spell book under a bright moon with lightning and smoke surrounding it. Diamond Tiara leaned over to Apple Bloom, Sweetie Belle, and Scootaloo.

"I know you all are the experts, but that cutie mark looks pretty ominous to me," she whispered. Apple Bloom didn't disagree, but she knew from experience that not every cutie mark meant what it seemed at first glance. You should never judge a book by its cover. Even if it has a creepy-looking cover.

Apple Bloom glanced at Scootaloo and Sweetie Belle, who seemed a little less excited about being the Ponyville Schoolhouse welcoming committee now that they had gotten a look at the new student. Apple Bloom cleared her throat to get their attention.

"Okay, y'all. Let's say hey!" Apple Bloom trotted over to the new student, trusting her friends to follow. The new student gazed at Apple Bloom, who smiled back and held out her hoof.

"Hey there! Welcome to Ponyville. I'm Apple Bloom. These are my friends, Scootaloo and Sweetie Belle."

"Hi," the new pony said without smiling as she studied the Crusaders. Apple Bloom thought she saw the pony's piercing eyes linger on their matching cutie marks.

"We call ourselves the Cutie Mark Crusaders," Apple Bloom continued, "because...well, that's a long story. But we wanted to welcome you to Ponyville!" Apple Bloom glanced at Sweetie Belle and Scootaloo, nodding at them to introduce themselves.

"Nice to meet you..." Scootaloo paused, waiting for the pony to introduce herself. "Um, do you have a name?"

"Lilymoon," the Unicorn said coolly.

She brushed past the Crusaders and took a seat at a desk, completely ignoring everypony in the room.

"Well," Sweetie Belle said, letting out a big breath. "She's sure friendly."

CHAPTER THREE

The school day passed quickly and uneventfully. Miss Cheerilee had just as little success engaging Lilymoon as the Crusaders did. Aside from repeating her name and stating that her family was from Trotsylvania, she remained silent the whole time.

Pip, Diamond Tiara, and a few others tried as well, but she would just stare at them with her piercing eyes and walk away. Determined to be friendly, Apple Bloom tried one more time at the end of the day. She headed over, planning to ask how Lilymoon's first day went, but the moment class was dismissed, Lilymoon jumped up and left quickly. Diamond Tiara and

Silver Spoon joined Apple Bloom on the steps of the Schoolhouse and watched Lilymoon hurry away.

"We're all trying our best to be welcoming," Diamond Tiara huffed, "but if a pony doesn't *want* to be friends with anypony else, far be it from me to force her!" Silver Spoon nodded in agreement and they both trotted off.

"Oh well." Scootaloo shrugged as she hopped down the Schoolhouse stairs. "Guess you can't make friends with everypony. What are we gonna do this afternoon?"

Apple Bloom had an idea. They could go the clubhouse and hang out just like they did yesterday and the day before and the day before. Back when they didn't have their cutie marks, they would spend hours making lists and coming up with schemes. But lately, they just hung out, discussed what had happened at school that day, and then headed home. At least Lilymoon was something new and different. Apple Bloom wondered why a pony would act so standoffish when they were all so obviously trying to make her feel welcome.

"You think maybe she just misses her friends back home?" Apple Bloom asked the others.

"Lilymoon?" Scootaloo laughed. "With an attitude like that, what makes you think she *has* any friends back home?"

"She gave me the creeps," Sweetie Belle added. "The way she stared at us? Spooky."

"Maybe things are different in Trotsylvania," Apple Bloom countered.

"Maybe starin' at ponies is the way they say hello?"

"Why are you trying so hard to defend her?" Scootaloo asked.

Apple Bloom thought for a moment. "I dunno," she answered honestly. "I guess I'm just trying to figure her out."

"Well, just ask her," Sweetie Belle suggested.

"I don't think she's gonna be any more talkative tomorrow," Scootaloo said.

"No," Sweetie Belle said, "I meant ask her right now." She pointed. "Look!"

Apple Bloom and Scootaloo both looked and saw Lilymoon sneaking down a path leading out of Ponyville directly toward the Everfree Forest! The Crusaders hid behind a bush and quietly watched her. Lilymoon peered around to make sure nopony was watching and then carefully stepped over the roots of a large tree into the dark woods.

"Why is she going into the Everfree Forest?" Sweetie Belle whispered.

"Well, there's one way to find out!" Apple Bloom whispered back. "Come on!"

"Why do we even care what the new pony is doing?" Scootaloo groaned.

Apple Bloom didn't answer. She leaped over the roots of the large tree and followed Lilymoon into the Forest. She caught a glimpse of a blue tail with a white streak disappearing behind some trees.

"This way, y'all!" she whispered. The others rushed after Apple Bloom, deeper into the Forest.

They tried their best to follow Lilymoon. But she was quick for a pony who had never explored the Everfree Forest before. After a few minutes, they accepted the fact that she was long gone.

"Why would a new pony go rushing off by herself into the Everfree Forest?" Apple Bloom wondered aloud. "What is she doing out here?"

"What are *we* doing out here?" Sweetie Belle asked, looking around the Forest. "It's gonna be dark soon."

"Yeah, are we done now?" Scootaloo asked.

"Crusaders," Apple Bloom said, turning to the others with a huge grin on her face, "somethin' mysterious is goin' on, and we're gonna find out what!"

CHAPTER FOUR

The next morning, Apple Bloom was determined to get some answers out of Lilymoon.

"We were being 'polite friendly' yesterday," Apple Bloom explained as they headed toward the Schoolhouse, "but today we're gonna get serious about being nice." Sweetie Belle and Scootaloo exchanged looks.

"You sure seem awful concerned about Lilymoon," Scootaloo observed.

"Well, it's like you said," Apple Bloom replied after considering for a second. "Maybe Lilymoon is the thing that came along when we least expected it. Maybe figurin' this out is something only we can do!"

"Do you maybe think you might be overreacting?" Sweetie Belle asked. "All we really know is she's kinda mean and wandered into the Everfree Forest. That's not *that* strange."

"I'm not overreactin'! I just think we should get to know more about her before something strange *does* happen." Apple Bloom walked up the steps of the Schoolhouse and stopped in her tracks.

"Uh. We might be a little late," Scootaloo said.

The inside of the Schoolhouse was an absolute disaster. Somepony had smeared paint all over the walls; stacks of books towered over the ponies, waving precariously back and forth but never quite tipping over; and all the desks and chairs were stuck to the ceiling! It looked like the Crusaders were the last ones to arrive. All the other students were pointing and talking over one another about the state of the classroom. Apple Bloom glanced around quickly, looking for Lilymoon. She saw her over in the corner by herself, observing the mess. Apple Bloom couldn't quite read her expression.

"Okay, let's all calm down," Miss Cheerilee announced, looking anything *but* calm. "Everypony take your seats, and we'll get to the bottom of this."

"Uh, Miss Cheerilee?" Snails motioned to the ceiling where all the seats in the classroom were currently stuck. Miss Cheerilee let out an exasperated sigh.

"Oh. Right. Okay, everypony just sit in the middle of the classroom and don't touch anything. I'm going to run and find Starlight Glimmer or Zecora or... somepony who can deal with...all this." As soon as Miss Cheerilee was gone, the ponies gathered in the center of the room and tried guessing what could have possibly happened.

"You think this is some kinda prank?" asked Silver Spoon.

"Well, if it ith, who did it?" demanded Twist.

"Forget who," said Scootaloo. "*How* did they do it?"

"Well, it *must* be a Unicorn." Diamond Tiara motioned to the desks and chairs above them. "This is *obviously* magic."

"That's a whole lotta magic for just a

prank!" said Snips. "I don't think *any* of us could do that. Could we?"

Apple Bloom glanced over her shoulder at Lilymoon, who was hanging back and not contributing to the conversation. Based on some of the looks the other ponies shot in Lilymoon's direction, Apple Bloom could tell she wasn't the only one who'd noticed. Pip wandered around the room examining the stacks of books.

"Well, whoever did it definitely took his or her time," Pip observed. "This must have taken all night!" Pip brushed too close to one of the stacks. It wobbled back and forth. "Oh bother," he muttered. Everypony gasped as the entire stack slowly teetered over and crashed onto the floor, sending books everywhere. The students looked around, but the other stacks remained standing, and the desks and chairs remained firmly on the ceiling. "Well, that wasn't too bad," Pip said, relieved.

One of the toppled books suddenly flew into the air. Diamond Tiara yelped. A second book flew up and slammed against the wall. Another book flew in the opposite direction, causing several ponies to duck. Something bumped Twist, knocking her backward. It was almost as if some invisible force were moving through the room, throwing books. Whatever it was, it was moving steadily in one direction.

It was moving right toward Pip!

CHAPTER FIVE

Pip backed away as the books flew into the air in a path that led toward him. He zigged and zagged out of the way, but no matter where he moved, the invisible force changed direction and continued toward him.

"Keep it away from me!" yelled Pip. Scootaloo rushed toward the books flying into the air but looked around, unsure what to do next.

"Keep *what* away? There's nothing here!" she exclaimed. The books stopped. Nopony moved a muscle.

Suddenly, Pip launched up toward the ceiling as if something had grabbed him by the hoof. He shouted in alarm as the classroom broke into pandemonium.

"*What's happening?!*" screamed Snips.

"*Run for your lives!*" yelled Snails.

"*Somepony get me down from here!*" Pip squealed as he flew through the air, weaving among the chairs and desks.

Apple Bloom searched the room for Lilymoon. She was standing out of the way in the corner, watching Pip intently. She took a step forward, as if she were about to do something.

But Sweetie Belle jumped in front of Apple Bloom, blocking her view. "We need to get him down from there!"

Apple Bloom watched Pip and got an idea. She turned to the others.

"Crusaders! Remember when we performed in the opening ceremonies of the Equestria Games?"

"Oh yeah!" Scootaloo said, grinning.

"I'm on it!" She ran to the back of the class to give herself some room. Sweetie Belle and Apple Bloom stood facing each other, their hooves outstretched between them. Scootaloo galloped toward her friends.

"One," counted Apple Bloom as Scootaloo leaped toward them.

"Two," Sweetie Belle continued as Scootaloo landed in her friends' hooves.

"Three!" Apple Bloom and Sweetie Belle said together as they hurled Scootaloo into the air.

Scootaloo flew through the classroom and slammed into Pip. Whatever had a hold of him let go, and they both flew into a pile of books, knocking the tower to the ground as they landed. Pip was a bit shaken up but otherwise unharmed.

Everypony rushed out of the
Schoolhouse toward the playground
and waited, silent and scared. But
whatever had grabbed Pip seemed to have
disappeared . . . for the moment, at least.

"Thith definitely theemth like more
than jutht a prank," observed Twist.

"Well, if nopony else is going to point
out the obvious, I will," Silver Spoon
announced. "Nothing like this has
ever happened before, so what's the big
difference now?"

Silver Spoon turned and glared at
Lilymoon, who was standing away from
the other ponies. "Would *you* like to tell us
anything, *Lilymoon*?" The students all glared
at Lilymoon, waiting for her to respond to
the accusation. She glared back at them.

"I have nothing to say to any of you,"

Lilymoon said defensively. Apple Bloom stepped forward.

"Now, everypony, just take a breath," Apple Bloom began. "Lilymoon, nopony is sayin' this is your fault or nothin'—"

"I think that's exactly what we're saying," Diamond Tiara interrupted. "You don't think it's a little bit odd that Lilymoon shows up, and the next thing you know, all *this* happens?"

"I ain't sayin' it's not odd," Apple Bloom said, "but this ain't the first crazy thing to ever happen in Ponyville. For all we know she could be just as confused as we are." She turned. "Lilymoon?"

Lilymoon glared at Apple Bloom. Instead of answering, she ran off.

Silver Spoon turned to Apple Bloom. "Looks pretty guilty to me."

CHAPTER SIX

Once Miss Cheerilee returned and heard what had happened to Pip, she announced that class was canceled and the Schoolhouse would be closed until they figured out just what was going on.

With the rest of the day free, the Cutie Mark Crusaders decided to head back to Sweet Apple Acres. Granny Smith was on a zap apple baking rampage, and the kitchen was bursting with baked goods. Apple Bloom knew there would be plenty to snack on while they discussed what to do about Lilymoon and the Schoolhouse. Apple Bloom, Sweetie Belle, and Scootaloo entered the kitchen to find Granny in the midst of baking a batch of zap apple pies to go along with the jams, tarts, muffins, and fritters that already filled the kitchen.

"Now hurry up and fix those pipes! I got another batch to make up for Golden Delicious after this'n!" Granny called out.

"Eeyup!" Big Mac replied from under the sink as he tinkered with the plumbing. Applejack walked into the kitchen carrying another bushel of zap apples. She set them down and wiped sweat from her brow.

"Here ya go, Granny," Applejack said. "This should do ya for the next coupla batches." Applejack saw the Crusaders in the kitchen and glanced up at the clock. "Hold up. Why aren't y'all in school?" she asked suspiciously.

"Miss Cheerilee let us out early today,"

Apple Bloom mentioned casually as she gathered some zap apple fritters to take up to her room. But her sister wasn't gonna let her off that easily.

"And why would Cheerilee let y'all out early?" Applejack pressed. "What happened?"

"Well, nopony knows *exactly* what happened," Scootaloo offered up. Apple Bloom shot her a look, but Scootaloo rolled her eyes and continued. "Something messed up the Schoolhouse. The whole place was a disaster. And then whatever did it grabbed Pip and flew him around the room!"

"Say *what*, now?!" Applejack exclaimed as Granny Smith and Big Mac stopped what they were doing to listen.

"A few of the ponies in class think the

new student has something to do with all of it. But we don't know that for sure yet," Sweetie Belle added.

"It's that new family up on Horseshoe Hill!" Granny Smith said. "That house has been empty for more moons than I care to count. Somethin' strange about it."

"Eeyup," Big Mac agreed.

"What's strange?" Apple Bloom asked.

"Well, nopony knows for sure," Granny said, placing some pies on the windowsill to cool. "But there's a reason it's been empty for so long. The ponies who lived there before...somethin' wasn't right about them, if I recall."

"Oh, that's just a buncha old ponies' tales," Applejack scoffed. She turned back to the Crusaders. "You said somethin' grabbed Pip and spun him? That sounds dangerous. Maybe I should head over to the castle, round up the others, and we can—"

"*No! It's fine!*" Apple Bloom said, louder than she intended. Everypony stopped and looked at her.

"Well, it don't sound fine to me," Applejack insisted, "and it won't hurt for me to mention to Twilight—"

"Ponies in Equestria *somehow* managed to survive before you and your friends came along, y'know!" Apple Bloom blurted out.

Applejack stared at her sister in surprise.

"Well, of course I know that. I'm just worried about you is all."

"Of *course* you're worried about me!" Apple Bloom said, rolling her eyes. "You're the almighty Applejack, hero of Equestria!

And I'm just your little sister who can't do anything on her own!" Apple Bloom stormed out of the kitchen and slammed the door, leaving a very confused Apple family—and the zap apple fritters—behind her.

Apple Bloom sat at a table inside Sugarcube Corner eating one of Mrs. Cake's cupcakes. It wasn't as good as anything Granny Smith was currently baking, but on the plus side, there was no annoying big sister here trying to do everything for her.

Apple Bloom heard the door open and knew without looking it was Scootaloo and Sweetie Belle. They both sat down at the table and waited a few minutes before saying anything.

"So"—Scootaloo finally broke the silence—"that was...interesting."

Apple Bloom was embarrassed. She hadn't planned on blowing up at her sister, especially in front of her friends. She knew

Applejack just wanted to help. But if her sister was gonna run around saving the day all the time, what did that leave for Apple Bloom to do?

"We got our cutie marks. We're not little fillies anymore," Apple Bloom explained. "When Applejack was my age, she had already defeated Nightmare Moon!"

"Actually," Scootaloo said, doing the math in her head, "I don't think they were *quite* this young when—"

"The point is," Apple Bloom interrupted, "helpin' other ponies find their cutie marks is nice and all, but…" She trailed off.

"But our sisters and their friends save Equestria every other day…" Sweetie Belle finished for her.

"Yeah," Apple Bloom agreed. "We got some big hooves to fill."

Scootaloo put her wing on Apple Bloom's shoulder. "Look, we get it. Sweetie Belle feels the same way being Rarity's sister, and everypony knows I wish I were half as awesome as Rainbow Dash. But comparing yourself to the most heroic ponies in Equestria, one of whom happens to be your sister, is a *lot* of pressure!"

"I know," Apple Bloom admitted, "but I guess I just figured this stuff with Lilymoon happened at *our* Schoolhouse. With a pony *our* age. I was hoping it was something we could handle ourselves."

Scootaloo and Sweetie Belle glanced at each other and nodded.

"Well then, let's handle it," Scootaloo said, grinning.

"Really?" Apple Bloom asked.

"I guess so," Sweetie Belle said a little

nervously. "I mean, if I'm gonna do something completely terrifying, I may as well do it with my two best friends, right?"

"We're the Cutie Mark Crusaders," Scootaloo said. "We've done everything together for as long as I can remember. So if you think figuring out what's going on with Lilymoon is our next big mission, then you can count on us!"

Apple Bloom hugged her friends. She really was the luckiest pony in the whole world.

"Well, let's go over what we know so far. Lilymoon's family is from Trotsylvania and they live up in that house on Horseshoe Hill. Granny said something was up with that place. Maybe we can start there?"

"*Or,*" Scootaloo said, slamming her hooves on the table, "we return to the scene of the crime!" She smiled triumphantly.

"The Schoolhouse?" Sweetie Belle asked.

"No! The Everfree Forest!" Scootaloo corrected.

"Technically, that's not the scene of the crime," Sweetie Belle said matter-of-factly. "That's just where we spotted her." While the two of them bickered, Apple Bloom glanced out the window.

"Ugh. You know what I mean!" Scootaloo rolled her eyes.

"I just don't know why it makes sense to—" Sweetie Belle began, but Apple Bloom interrupted her.

"Scootaloo, you're a genius!" Apple Bloom announced.

"I am?" Scootaloo asked. Apple Bloom pointed. Sweetie Belle and Scootaloo looked out the window and, sure enough, there was Lilymoon, sneaking right back into the Everfree Forest!

"We can't just go rushing after her like we did last time," Apple Bloom said to the others as they hurried out of Sugarcube Corner.

"Well, what do you suggest? She's already got a head start," Scootaloo said impatiently.

Apple Bloom looked ahead. She could see Lilymoon was headed toward the same tree with the same big roots she had climbed over yesterday. If they just rushed after her, they would probably lose her again. Apple Bloom examined the options. She saw a larger entrance nearby with a clearer path.

"There!" Apple Bloom pointed. "We

can enter the Forest through there so we don't have to go crawling through the trees and bushes. It will let us get a little bit ahead, and then we can wait for her!" The other two nodded, and they veered toward the entrance.

"And we're *sure* this is how we want to spend our afternoon?" Sweetie Belle asked one more time.

"Yes!" Apple Bloom insisted.

They entered the Forest and ran as quickly as they could down the path. Once she thought they were far enough ahead, Apple Bloom motioned for the other two to slow down. They stopped and listened. Sure enough, in addition to the usual spooky sounds of the Forest, they could hear somepony walking through bushes and making just enough noise to be heard.

"This way, y'all," Apple Bloom whispered as she stepped off the path and picked her way carefully through the overgrown Forest. After all, it wouldn't do them any good if Lilymoon heard them coming.

As they got farther away from the path, Apple Bloom quickly realized that, as many times as the Crusaders had been in the Everfree Forest (and they had been in there more often than most), they had *never* been in this particular part before. Apple Bloom recalled Zecora had once mentioned that the Forest was much bigger than most ponies realized, even ponies who thought they understood the Everfree Forest. Apple Bloom was beginning to appreciate just how little she actually knew about it. Something about this part of the

Forest seemed wilder, more dangerous than the parts she knew (and those parts were no trot in the park!).

Up ahead, she saw what looked like a clearing and heard what she hoped was Lilymoon. She motioned to Scootaloo and Sweetie Belle, and the three of them crept up to a large tree with vines hanging from its branches. They brushed the vines to the side and peered slowly around the tree.

Lilymoon stood in the clearing. She was using her horn to levitate large rocks and stack them on top of one another.

"Look!" whispered Sweetie Belle. "It's *just* like the books in the Schoolhouse!"

"She *was* the one doing it," replied Scootaloo.

"But why's she doin' it out here?" whispered Apple Bloom.

Lilymoon continued stacking rocks and glancing around the Forest, as if she were expecting somepony to show up.

Apple Bloom took a step forward to get a closer look and stepped on a twig. It was small and made the tiniest snap, but it was enough to get Lilymoon's attention. She turned toward the Crusaders and stared at Apple Bloom, surprised.

"Lilymoon, we got a couple of questions for you," Apple Bloom said sternly as she stepped toward her. "Right, y'all?"

"Mmpph mph MMMMPH," she heard behind her. Apple Bloom turned.

Sweetie Belle and Scootaloo were wrapped up in vines. Their mouths were covered and they were being pulled slowly up into the branches of the tree!

"Lilymoon! *Stop it!*" Apple Bloom yelled, but when she turned, Lilymoon was gone! In a panic, Apple Bloom rushed toward the tree. She jumped up to grab her friends, but they were already too high to reach. She wasn't sure what to do! She looked around frantically, but there was nothing nearby she could use to reach them. So instead, she did what any Apple family member in her position would do. She started bucking the tree. Hard.

"*Put!*" **Buck.** "*My!*" **Buck.** "*Friends!*" **Buck.** "*Down!*" **Buck.** Surprisingly, this actually had an effect. The vines around

Sweetie Belle and Scootaloo loosened enough for them to get their mouths free.

"It's working!" Scootaloo yelled. "Keep hitting it!" Apple Bloom reared back her hooves when she felt something down near the ground. She looked and saw more vines wrapping themselves around her. The vines tugged and, with a scream, Apple Bloom was pulled up into the air to join the others.

"This is really bad." Sweetie Belle groaned.

"It's not *that* bad," said Apple Bloom as she tried unsuccessfully to grab on to a branch to stop her steady ascent.

"Not that bad?!" Sweetie Belle exclaimed. "A giant tree is pulling us to our doom and nopony even knows we're out here! How could it get any worse?!"

A noise caught the Crusaders' attention and they all turned to see Lilymoon standing nearby, watching the tree pull them higher and higher.

"Well," said Scootaloo, "*somepony* knows where we are." She glared down at Lilymoon. "So this is your plan? We catch you doing...whatever it is you're doing out here, so you have this tree attack us? We're the Cutie Mark Crusaders! We're gonna get out of this easily!" Scootaloo struggled harder, but the vines around them tightened.

Lilymoon didn't say anything. Instead, she rushed over to the trunk of the tree and started feeling around with her hooves. Whatever she was doing caused the tree to pull up the vines faster, as if it was in a hurry to do whatever it planned to do to the ponies.

"Lilymoon, *please!*" shouted Apple Bloom. "You don't have to do this!" Lilymoon ignored Apple Bloom as she continued searching around with her hooves. She reached underneath a lower branch and the entire tree shuddered. She pressed harder and the tree began to sway back and forth. The Crusaders all screamed as they rocked along with the tree. Lilymoon looked up one last time before rushing off into the Forest.

"*Great!*" Scootaloo yelled. "She sics her tree on us and takes off! What now?"

"*Help us! Anypony!*" Sweetie Belle yelled. Scootaloo and Apple Bloom joined in.

"*We're being eaten by a tree!*" Scootaloo yelled.

The tree continued swaying. As it did, the vines around the ponies loosened. They quickly became loose enough for the ponies to untangle themselves. Apple Bloom, Scootaloo, and Sweetie Belle jumped down and ran a safe distance away before turning back to watch the swaying tree. As they did, the tree slowed its back-and-forth motion until it eventually once again stood still. The vines dropped and hung innocently, but the Crusaders now knew better than to approach it.

"Why did it let us go?" Sweetie Belle asked.

"I bet our yelling scared it," Scootaloo said confidently.

"Seriously?" Sweetie Belle asked. "I don't think three ponies scared out of their minds screaming for help stopped the hungry tree."

"Lilymoon left," Apple Bloom said,

looking in the direction she ran. "As soon as she was gone, the tree stopped attacking us. She was doing it."

"Yeah! Because we know she's the one who messed up the Schoolhouse and attacked Pip!" Scootaloo said angrily.

"Should we go tell somepony? Like, maybe our sisters?" Sweetie Belle asked.

"No," Apple Bloom insisted. "We're goin' to Lilymoon's house on Horseshoe Hill and we are gonna get to the bottom of this."

"I knew that's what you were gonna say," Sweetie Belle said with a heavy sigh.

CHAPTER TEN

If Diamond Tiara hadn't told the Cutie Mark Crusaders where the house on Horseshoe Hill was, Apple Bloom was sure they never would have found it. Now that she was looking at it, she recognized it was by far one of the largest houses in Ponyville. But it was so tucked out of the way that she had probably passed it hundreds of times in her life and never noticed it. Ponyville and the Everfree Forest were right next to each other, but there was usually a clear division where one ended and the other began. High on the hilltop, the house blended into the Forest, almost like it was a part of it. Vines wrapped around the walls of the five-story cottage. Trees grew right next to it and branches brushed against the windows. The cottage itself seemed to be somehow wilder than other buildings in Ponyville.

"Wow," Scootaloo said, studying the house. "That is definitely the..."

"Scariest house in Ponyville?" Sweetie Belle finished. "Yeah, definitely the scariest house in Ponyville."

"It's *just* a house, y'all," Apple Bloom insisted. "Now, let's go get a better look." The ponies crept up the hill, careful to stay close to the trees and bushes so they wouldn't be spotted by anypony. They crept even closer to the house. The vines growing up against the wall wrapped tightly around the windows.

"Great," Sweetie Belle muttered, "more vines." Apple Bloom rolled her eyes and pushed the vines out of the way with her hoof. Through the window, they could see what looked like a workroom. There were jars filled with all kinds of things, strange plants lining the walls, lab equipment set out on tables, and two Unicorns—one male, one female—wearing goggles and standing next to a large cauldron. They had the same lavender complexion, blue mane, and piercing violet eyes as Lilymoon.

"Do you think those are Lilymoon's parents?" Scootaloo whispered. Apple Bloom shushed her and kept watching. One of the Unicorns, the male, poured vials filled with different liquids into the cauldron. The other Unicorn plucked leaves off a nearby plant and dropped them into the mixture as well. The cauldron bubbled violently as purple smoke poured out onto the floor.

"What kinda potion *is* that?" Apple Bloom wondered aloud. She squinted. It was getting harder to see what was going on; the window was so foggy.

"Uh. Apple Bloom?" Scootaloo tapped her with her hoof. Apple Bloom turned and realized it wasn't just the window getting foggy. A mist had come out of nowhere and surrounded them! Apple Bloom and the others tried to back away from the window, but their hooves stuck to the ground as if it were made of taffy.

"*Gross!*" Scootaloo yelled as her hooves sank into the ground.

"I can't move!" Sweetie Belle squeaked as she tried in vain to back away from the window. A chuckle echoed around them, but they couldn't see anypony through the fog.

"Wh-who's there?" Apple Bloom asked. "What do you want?"

"What do I want?" a crackly voice asked with another chuckle. "I'm not the one snooping into other ponies' business, now, am I?" A glowing horn appeared as the fog swirled away, revealing an old Unicorn. She was at least as old as Granny Smith (if not older) and had a tangled gray mess of a mane. She studied the Crusaders carefully. "Auntie Eclipse thinks you should answer your own question. What do *you* want?"

Before anypony could answer, an explosion from inside the house engulfed them all in smoke.

In the commotion after the blast, Apple Bloom realized she could move her hooves again. She could hear Auntie Eclipse coughing and didn't waste any time. She turned to run in the opposite direction.

"Run, y'all! This way!" she yelled. Scootaloo and Sweetie Belle followed her, leaving the old Unicorn behind them.

"I can't see anything!" Sweetie Belle called.

"This way! Follow my voice!" Apple Bloom shouted back. The purple fog was beginning to clear up and Apple Bloom could just make out the path they had taken that would lead them back to Ponyville. But before she could get there, another Unicorn jumped in her way, blocking them.

"Over here, Auntie!" she yelled. The fog had cleared enough for Apple Bloom to see the pony clearly. She was slightly older than the Crusaders and looked like Lilymoon but in reverse. A blue coat, a lavender tail, and a lavender mane with a single black streak running through it. She lowered her head and her horn glowed brightly, lifting the Crusaders off the ground.

"Hey! *Let us down!*" Scootaloo yelled. The Unicorn's horn glowed again and the Crusaders suddenly found they were unable to speak!

"Well done, Ambermoon!" Auntie Eclipse said as she walked slowly toward them. "Now we can get some answers!"

"Is everypony okay?" The female

Unicorn with the goggles came rushing out of the house. She saw Auntie Eclipse and the other Unicorn, Ambermoon, with the floating Crusaders. "What's going on out here?" she asked cautiously.

"Well, *that* didn't work," the male pony said as he walked outside. "We're *never* going to be able to break into the Livewood if we—"

"Blue Moon!" the female Unicorn said loudly, interrupting his thought mid-sentence. "We have intruders!" The male Unicorn, Blue Moon, raised his goggles and studied the Crusaders.

"Intruders? They're just—"

"Sticking their snouts where they don't belong!" Auntie Eclipse insisted. She turned to the Crusaders. "Now, who are you and what are you—"

"Auntie!" Ambermoon gasped. "Look!" Auntie Eclipse and the others followed Ambermoon's gaze. She was staring at the Crusaders' matching cutie marks.

"Well, look at that," Blue Moon whispered. He studied the Crusaders with renewed interest. "Who in Equestria are the three of you?"

"I know who they are," said a voice from the doorstep. Everypony turned to see Lilymoon standing there. "They go to my school. I'll deal with them."

"You didn't mention you were going to have guests," the female Unicorn with the goggles said.

"Sorry, Mother," Lilymoon said calmly, her eyes never leaving the Crusaders. "It must have slipped my mind." Lilymoon's mother nodded to Ambermoon. Her horn flashed as she released the Crusaders, dropping them gently to the ground. Lilymoon's mother looked down at them, her eyes darting to their cutie marks.

"I'm Lumi Nation, Lily's mother." She didn't smile as she spoke. In fact, she didn't seem particularly friendly at all. "This is her father, Blue Moon; her sister, Ambermoon; and our aunt Eclipse." Each of the Unicorns nodded to the Crusaders. "Lilymoon doesn't often bring friends around. We apologize for any confusion."

"No problem," Apple Bloom said, watching Lilymoon carefully as she spoke. "We just wanted to stop by and . . . see how you all were liking Ponyville so far."

"It's a little too nosy for my taste," Auntie Eclipse muttered. A look from Lumi Nation quieted her. Blue Moon grinned widely at the Crusaders, like he was trying a bit too hard to be friendly.

"Personally, I find Ponyville *full* of surprises," he said. "For example, I see you all have matching cutie marks. That's definitely...different." The entire family looked at the Crusaders expectantly.

"Yeah. It's actually pretty awesome." Scootaloo showed off her cutie mark. "Ponies are always interested, since we've got the only matching cutie marks in Equestria."

"I wouldn't be so sure about that," Auntie Eclipse whispered. Apple Bloom looked more closely at Lilymoon's family's cutie marks. Where Lilymoon had her spell book, Ambermoon had a potion bottle, Lumi Nation had a leaf, and Blue Moon had a star. But on top of those symbols, they each had the exact same bright moon, smoke, and lightning. Lilymoon's family had matching cutie marks, *just* like the Cutie Mark Crusaders!

CHAPTER TWELVE

Despite Lilymoon's family wanting to know absolutely *everything* about the CMCs and their matching cutie marks, Lilymoon convinced them she needed to talk to her "friends" alone. She brought the Crusaders into Auntie Eclipse's library. There were some old and dusty chairs, tables, and couches scattered throughout the room. A large map of Equestria hung on one wall. Below it was an equally large map of what looked like the Everfree Forest. There were strange artifacts lying around, and of course, most of the room was filled ceiling to floor with shelves of ancient-looking books. Lilymoon slid the library door closed and turned to glare at the Crusaders.

"What are you doing here?" she asked.

"We'll ask the questions!" Scootaloo said aggressively. "We saw what you were doing with those rocks in the Forest! *Just* like the books in the Schoolhouse! We caught you red-hooved! Don't try to deny it!"

"You don't know what you're talking about," Lilymoon responded flatly.

"Oh yeah? Then why did you have your tree attack us?" Scootaloo demanded.

Lilymoon snorted and rolled her eyes. "I saved the three of you from that Poison Joke Tree because you obviously have *no* idea how to take care of yourselves in the Forest."

"Poison Joke Tree? I thought Poison Joke was on the ground," Sweetie Belle said.

Apple Bloom wasn't sure what to think.

Lilymoon sighed. "Poison Joke *also* grows on trees. It's rare. But it happens. The vines pull you up until the leaves infect you. The only way to get free is to find the tree's ticklish spot."

"You were *tickling* the tree?!" Sweetie Belle asked incredulously. "You saved us?"

"Of course I did." Lilymoon arched an eyebrow. "I wasn't going to let you get hurt just because you were spying on me."

"We were spying on you because of what you did in the Schoolhouse!" Apple Bloom shot back.

"I wasn't the one who did that to the Schoolhouse!" Lilymoon said angrily. But then her face fell and she looked away.

"But I *am* still the one who's responsible," she added quietly.

"Say what, now?" Apple Bloom asked.

Lilymoon studied the Crusaders as if she was weighing her options. "It was a bogle," she finally said.

"What's a bogle?" asked Scootaloo.

"A bogle is a creature that lives deep in forests. They're very rare. Just like Poison Joke Trees." Lilymoon's cold exterior melted *slightly* as she explained things.

"Are they scary-looking?" asked Sweetie Belle.

"Nopony knows exactly what they look like. They're invisible," Lilymoon explained. "In fact, there's a *lot* ponies don't know about them." She walked over to one of the bookshelves and searched. "That's why my family moved here," she added.

"For bogles?" asked Apple Bloom.

"No," Lilymoon said as she searched, "to be closer to the Everfree Forest. It's kind of an obsession, to be honest. There's just so much ponies don't know about it. Here!" She used her horn to levitate a book off the shelf, placing it on a nearby table.

"*The Lost Creatures of Equestria*," she read as she blew dust off the cover. "This book contains the only recorded mention of bogles." Lilymoon flipped through the book until she came to the page she was looking for.

" 'Bogles tend to keep to themselves,' " she read. " 'They're very territorial and mark their nests with elaborate decoration. Methods can include but are not limited to: scratching symbols in trees, bright colors, stacking and levitation of objects—basically anything that makes their nest look as unique as possible. They get furious if anything disturbs their home.'" Lilymoon looked down at her hooves. "I wanted to observe a bogle in its natural habitat. I found the nest when I went into the Forest after school, but the bogle wasn't there. I went back and checked again this morning. I didn't think it was there. I should have been more careful.... I knocked over a couple of rocks...."

She sighed and then continued reading. "'Once provoked, the bogle abandons its nest and tracks the creature who disturbed it. It builds a new nest in the victim's home. If it likes its new surroundings more than its old nest, it's almost impossible to force it to leave.'" Lilymoon looked at the Crusaders. "I got to the Schoolhouse early.

So did the bogle. I think it *really* likes the Schoolhouse."

"Wow. So this really *was* all your fault!" Scootaloo blurted out. Lilymoon looked away, embarrassed.

"Okay, okay," Apple Bloom said. "No use cryin' over spilled cider. How do we get rid of it?"

"That's the problem," Lilymoon said, flipping to the next page. "It doesn't say anything else about bogles. I was hoping when class started, all the noise would scare it off. But that obviously didn't happen. So I tried rebuilding its old nest, hoping it would miss it and return. But I don't think it wants to leave the Schoolhouse." She looked at the Crusaders, and for the first time she wasn't glaring at them. She seemed scared. "I don't think there *is* a way to get rid of it!"

CHAPTER THIRTEEN

"There has to be *some* way to get rid of it!" Scootaloo insisted. "This is your aunt's library, right? Maybe we could ask her?"

"No!" Lilymoon said firmly. "We can't do that!"

"Why not?" Sweetie Belle asked.

"Because." Lilymoon glanced back, making sure the door to the foyer was still closed. "I'm not supposed to go out into the Forest without them."

"So what were you doin' out there?" Apple Bloom asked. Lilymoon sat down in one of the ancient chairs, and a cloud of dust flew around her.

"My father is an expert on reading the stars. Astrology, science, magic. My mother spent her life studying the plants of Equestria. She can recognize every leaf, root, branch, and berry that exists, especially the ones with magical properties. My sister is a natural with potions and spells, and Auntie Eclipse...well...she knows everything about anything that has ever happened in Equestria."

"They sound smart! Why don't we want to ask them how to get rid of the bogle again?" Sweetie Belle asked, confused.

"I can hear exactly what they would say." Lilymoon groaned. *"Oh, Lilymoon, you shouldn't have gone out alone. Oh, Lilymoon, don't mess with things you don't understand. Oh, Lilymoon, why can't you be brilliant and amazing just like the rest of us? Oh, Lilymoon, why are you such a disappointment?"* Lilymoon frowned at the Crusaders. "My family has very high expectations. I was exploring the forests of Trotsylvania with my mother when I got my cutie mark. We were studying the flight patterns of perytons."

"What's a peryton?" asked Scootaloo.

"Not now!" scolded Apple Bloom. She nodded to Lilymoon to continue.

"I wasn't sure what a book had to do with magical creatures. I thought maybe I was supposed to study and catalog them. That's why I was trying to study the bogle. I don't know. I just want to show my family I'm good at something. You all wouldn't understand."

"Actually," Apple Bloom said, "I think we have a pretty good idea of what it's like to want to figure out what you're good at and prove yourself to ponies you look up to."

"You do?" Lilymoon asked.

"Definitely." Apple Bloom turned to the others. "So, Crusaders? What do ya say?"

"I say we're gonna come up with a plan to catch a bogle," Scootaloo said.

"I say I'm gonna regret everything about this," Sweetie Belle said with a groan.

Lilymoon stared at the Crusaders. She looked confused. "Why would you help me?" she asked.

"That's what friends do," Apple Bloom responded simply.

"I don't have friends," Lilymoon replied.

"Well, with that attitude, I can see why," Scootaloo fired back. Apple Bloom shot her a look. "What?" Scootaloo asked innocently.

"She's right," Lilymoon admitted. "I don't know if you noticed, but my family isn't exactly 'warm and fuzzy.' I guess I've always come across a little different. So nopony ever asked to be my friend and I never tried."

"Well, you got three friends now," Apple Bloom said. "And we're gonna help you fix this."

"Thank you," Lilymoon said, relief flooding her face.

"Now," Apple Bloom said, "let's think this through." She paced back and forth. "You said bogles like decorating their nests, right?" Lilymoon nodded. "And they *hate* when anypony disturbs them?"

"Pip found that out the hard way," Scootaloo reminded them.

"Well then, the first part of the plan is easy. We mess up the Schoolhouse and make the bogle mad," Apple Bloom said to the others.

"That is a *terrible* plan." Sweetie Belle groaned. "I don't know about you ponies, but I would prefer *not* to be grabbed by my hooves and tossed around the room by an invisible monster."

"He would have to catch us first," Scootaloo said confidently.

"That could work," Lilymoon said, "but *then* what? It didn't leave the Schoolhouse last time. I think it likes it too much in there!"

"Yeah, but if we had somewhere better we could lead it . . ." Scootaloo thought aloud.

"It's gonna have to be *reallllly* nice to convince it to leave," Lilymoon pointed out.

"Well, no offense, but your rock stacks weren't all that impressive," Scootaloo responded. They all sat and thought about it.

"Maybe the bogle is just tired of living in the woods?" Sweetie Belle suggested.

"How does that help us?" Scootaloo asked, rolling her eyes. "Unless you wanna let it live with you and Rarity?"

"No way!" Sweetie Belle squeaked. "Rarity loves her boutique. And she's scary when you mess with her stuff."

"Wait a minute!" Apple Bloom exclaimed. "I bet the bogle would love Rarity's stuff, too! It's way prettier than rocks and sticks in the woods!"

"What? No!" Sweetie Belle squealed nervously. "We are *not* setting a bogle loose in my sister's shop!"

"Of course not," Apple Bloom said. "But we *are* gonna need to borrow some of her stuff. Here's what we're gonna do..."

The Ponyville Schoolhouse, which was so welcoming during the day, looked incredibly creepy at night. *Of course*, thought Apple Bloom, *that might be because we know there is an invisible monster lurking inside.* The ponies hid in the bushes by the playground and looked warily at the school.

"Everything is set up. This is it. Is everypony ready?" Apple Bloom asked.

"*Why* are we doing this at night, again?" Sweetie Belle replied nervously.

"For the *hundredth* time, we are doing it at night because we don't want an invisible bogle knocking over every single pony in Ponyville during the day!" Scootaloo said.

"Okay, okay," Sweetie Belle muttered. "Doesn't make it any less scary!"

"We have the paint?" Apple Bloom asked.

"Yes." Lilymoon nodded toward the bag next to her.

"I just hope Rarity doesn't notice everything we borrowed," Sweetie Belle said.

"It's for a good cause," Apple Bloom reminded her. The ponies all sat in the bushes, none of them moving.

"Maybe we should go check everything in the Forest one more time?" Sweetie Belle suggested.

"No more stallin'. It's time to get in there," Apple Bloom said. "Let's go." The ponies all crawled out of the bushes and approached the Schoolhouse. They crept up the steps toward the front door. It was chained shut with a giant padlock on it.

"Oh well. Guess that's that," Sweetie Belle said, turning to walk down the steps. Scootaloo stopped her while Apple Bloom and Lilymoon studied the lock.

"Think you can pick it?" Apple Bloom asked.

"I don't know how to pick a lock!" Lilymoon said, annoyed.

"Hey, guys!" Scootaloo whispered.

"Can't you use magic?" Apple Bloom whispered.

"Guys!" Scootaloo said louder.

"I don't know that kind of magic," Lilymoon insisted.

"*Guys!*" Scootaloo called. Apple Bloom and Lilymoon turned. Scootaloo and

Sweetie Belle were standing next to one of the Schoolhouse windows. Scootaloo slid it open. "Not *every*thing needs to be super complicated. Come on!" Apple Bloom and Lilymoon hurried down the stairs with the bag of supplies and followed Scootaloo and Sweetie Belle through the window and into the Schoolhouse.

The Schoolhouse was dark. Even with Lilymoon and Sweetie Belle lighting their horns, it was still hard to see. The books were all restacked in precarious arches, each book carefully placed. The desks and chairs had been removed from the ceiling and now magically lined the sides of the walls. In their place, pictures drawn by the students plastered the ceiling in strange patterns. Miss Cheerilee's desk was in the center of the Schoolhouse, upside down on the floor. The curtains from the windows were placed in swirling shapes around it. Apple Bloom's ears perked up.

"*Shhhh.* Y'all hear that?" she asked. The ponies listened quietly. Steady breathing was coming from the center of the room.

"Is the bogle snoring?" Scootaloo asked. Apple Bloom nodded. She motioned to the bag next to Scootaloo.

"Get ready," Apple Bloom whispered. Scootaloo reached in and pulled out two cans of paint. She handed one to Lilymoon and held on to the other one.

"Ready," Scootaloo whispered back. Apple Bloom nodded to Sweetie Belle, who nervously rushed over to one side of the classroom while Apple Bloom headed to the other side. Scootaloo and Lilymoon quietly carried the cans of paint as close as they dared to Miss Cheerilee's desk. Everypony turned to watch Apple Bloom for the signal. Apple Bloom gulped and quickly wondered if Applejack was ever this scared when she was saving Equestria. She pushed the thought aside and looked to make sure everypony was ready.

"*Now!*" Apple Bloom yelled. She kicked hard, knocking over the stack of books closest to her. Sweetie Belle leaped onto one of the chairs stuck to the wall and pried it down. It fell to the ground with a loud crash. The snoring in the center of the room stopped. Scootaloo and Lilymoon both heaved the paint cans. Pink and purple paint flew through the room and landed on...something.

That very scary *something* covered in pink and purple paint rose slowly and let out a ferocious roar. The bogle was awake.

CHAPTER FIFTEEN

"I think we made it mad!" Scootaloo yelled as she kicked over another pile of books.

"Ya think?!" Apple Bloom called back. "Keep it up! We need to make sure it's really, really mad!" The ponies rushed around the room, destroying as much as they could while avoiding the angry bogle. Apple Bloom couldn't make out all the details (the bogle was still invisible), but thanks to the pink and purple paint, she could see it was a little bit smaller than Big Mac and had horns on top of its head; massive arms; long, spindly legs; and a powerful spiked tail. No wonder it was invisible. It was ugly!

"Okay, the first part of the plan worked!" Sweetie Belle squealed as the bogle rushed toward her. It tried to grab her, but she ran between its legs. "Can we get to the second part now? *Please?!*"

"Everypony out the window!" Apple Bloom yelled. The ponies all rushed toward the front of the Schoolhouse. They dived through the open window and landed in a heap in the bushes below.

"It's coming!" Lilymoon grunted. The ponies untangled themselves and ran across the playground. Apple Bloom looked back over her shoulder just in time to see the bogle crash through the front door of the Schoolhouse, easily breaking the chain and lock.

"Miss Cheerilee is *not* gonna like that!" Sweetie Belle wailed.

"At least the monster isn't *in* the Schoolhouse anymore!" Scootaloo said. "That's progress!" They ran toward the bushes, and Scootaloo brushed some leaves and branches aside, revealing her scooter.

"Okay, Scootaloo, you go ahead and make sure everything's ready," Apple Bloom ordered. "We'll be right behind you!"

Scootaloo nodded as she put on a headlamp and jumped onto her scooter. She sped off into the darkness.

Apple Bloom turned to see the bogle knock aside the playground's seesaw as it rushed toward them. She nodded at the others and they took off in the same direction as Scootaloo, the bogle close behind them.

They rushed through the empty streets of Ponyville, always turning back to make sure the bogle was following. Apple Bloom looked ahead and could see the edge of the Everfree Forest and the path the Crusaders had used earlier to follow Lilymoon. She couldn't believe that had been just this afternoon! When she woke up this morning she never would have guessed she would end the day being chased through the center of town by an invisible monster.

"Come on, y'all! The Forest is just over there!" Apple Bloom called. They rushed toward the path. Behind them, the bogle knocked over carts and took chunks out of several buildings as it rushed to catch them.

Apple Bloom hoped her plan would work. She didn't want to find out what the bogle was going to do to them if they failed.

Apple Bloom ran as fast as she could next to Lilymoon and Sweetie Belle, their horns the only source of light now that the moon and stars were blocked by the leafy canopy of the Everfree Forest.

"You sure this is the right way?" Lilymoon asked Apple Bloom.

"I think so?" Apple Bloom said, squinting into the darkness.

"Look! Over there!" Sweetie Belle shouted. Apple Bloom saw a bright light ahead of them. She and the others rushed toward it.

The ponies raced into the clearing where Lilymoon had originally found the bogle. Only now, it was completely transformed!

It didn't look anything like it had earlier in the day. Lanterns hung from tree branches, bathing the clearing in a warm, cozy glow. Fabrics of every color and pattern were stretched between the trees, creating a colorful tapestry that flowed gently in the breeze. Rocks were arranged carefully in swirling patterns on the ground, and in the center of all of it, piles of cloth were organized into an inviting nest.

"Psssssst!" A voice from above caught Apple Bloom's attention. She looked up to see Scootaloo waving to them from the branches of a tree. Apple Bloom, Sweetie Belle, and Lilymoon rushed up to join her. They all quietly watched the clearing below.

The paint-covered bogle burst into the clearing, expecting to find a bunch of scared ponies. Instead, it found its transformed nest. It stopped, looking around, confused. It growled menacingly as it slowly circled the clearing. It brushed its tail along the cloth and gently tapped the lanterns, watching them sway back and forth. It studied the patterns of the rocks on the ground, tapping each one with a claw as it passed.

"I think it's working," Scootaloo whispered.

"*Shhhhh!* Quiet!" Sweetie Belle hissed.

The bogle tested the nest of fabrics in the center of the clearing. It sniffed them, rearranged them, sniffed them again, and finally plopped down and burrowed into them.

"I think the bogle likes its old nest again," Lilymoon said.

"Well, as my sister would say, you can't

argue with good taste," Sweetie Belle added. Below them, the bogle purred happily. Rocks floated magically into the air as the bogle rearranged them into new patterns.

"*Awww.* It's kinda cute when it's not roaring and chasing you," Scootaloo said, grinning.

."Uh. *One* question," Sweetie Belle whispered to the others. "Now that the bogle is happy . . . how are we getting out of this tree?" The ponies all looked at one another.

"I guess we gotta wait for it to go back to sleep?" Apple Bloom said.

"That's what I was afraid you were gonna say," Sweetie Belle said, yawning. She and the others settled in as comfortably as they could to wait for the bogle to go to bed.

CHAPTER SEVENTEEN

Apple Bloom didn't remember falling asleep. But she must have, because the next thing she could remember was waking up to Sweetie Belle gently nudging her with her hoof.

"I think it's safe," Sweetie Belle whispered. Apple Bloom peered sleepily down at the bogle's nest. Some of Rarity's fabric was magically hovering in the air over the bogle's nest. It was curled up underneath them, still covered in paint, and snoring loudly.

"Those lanterns are brighter than they were before," Apple Bloom said with another yawn.

"That's not the lanterns," Scootaloo

said. Apple Bloom blinked a few times and realized the warm glow wasn't coming from the lanterns but instead from the sky in the east.

"Oh Celestia! We've been out all night!" Apple Bloom yelped loudly enough that the bogle below snorted and stirred. The ponies all froze until it resumed its snoring. Apple Bloom and the others carefully crawled out of the tree and slowly snuck around the edge of the bogle's nest, careful not to disturb anything. Once they were a good distance away, Sweetie Belle turned to the others.

"Do you think that's it?" she asked. "It's just gonna stay there?"

"I *think* so," Lilymoon said slowly. "Everything I read made it sound like if a bogle loves its nest, it just wants to be left alone. I think as long as nopony goes looking for it again, we should be fine."

"Let's hope so," Apple Bloom said as they walked out of the Everfree Forest into Ponyville.

"Uh-oh," Scootaloo said. The Crusaders and Lilymoon watched as ponies rushed around, shouting and examining the destruction left by the bogle. Scootaloo turned to the others. "You think we're gonna get in trouble for this?"

"There you are!" a voice called from up ahead. Apple Bloom saw Applejack marching toward her, Granny Smith and Big Mac close behind.

"Eeyup," Apple Bloom said.

"We've been worried *sick*! Where in the name of Celestia have y'all been all night?" Applejack shouted as she marched toward the Crusaders. Before Apple Bloom could answer, another voice broke through the crowd.

"*Lilymoon! What have you done?*" Lumi Nation shouted as she and Blue Moon came bursting through the crowd.

"Hey, y'all..." Apple Bloom said. "So, what happened was—"

"I went into the Everfree Forest by myself and a bogle followed me out," Lilymoon admitted, stepping in front of Apple Bloom. "That's what attacked the school. I'm to blame. The Cutie Mark Crusaders helped me lure it back into the Forest where it wouldn't hurt anypony." Lilymoon turned to Apple Bloom. "I couldn't have done it without...my friends." Lilymoon's parents' eyes went wide.

"A bogle?" her father asked. "Really?"

"Tell us everything," her mother said. "How did you lure it? What did it look like? Oh, darling, I'm so impressed!"

"Impressed?!" Granny Smith blurted out. "I'd be more impressed if she'd leave dangerous monsters alone in the first place." Lilymoon's parents glanced at the Apple family and shared a look.

"Yes. Well. We need to get Lilymoon home," Lumi Nation said curtly.

"We apologize for any problems this might have caused," Blue Moon said. "We will keep a closer eye on Lily. No need to bother her. Come, Lilymoon!" Her parents turned and walked off. Lilymoon obediently followed but looked back and mouthed the words *thank you* to the Crusaders as she walked away.

"Yeah," Scootaloo said, "there's definitely something strange about that family." Sweetie Belle and Apple Bloom nodded. Applejack looked down at Apple Bloom.

"Is what she said true?" Applejack asked. "You went and helped her catch this bogle thing she set loose?"

"Yeah," Apple Bloom replied.

"And why didn't you ask for my help?" Applejack looked more hurt than angry.

"Because..." Apple Bloom glanced at Scootaloo and Sweetie Belle, who nodded encouragingly. She turned to Applejack. "You're my big sister and I love you, but you save Equestria, like, every other day. I just wanted to show you I can be as brave as you are." Apple Bloom looked down sheepishly. Applejack studied her sister thoughtfully.

"Now listen," Applejack finally said. "You are one of the bravest ponies I've ever met in my life...and I know some pretty brave ponies. But you're also my little sister. I'm always gonna worry about you, and I'm always gonna want to help you. It don't mean I think you can't help yourself. It's just what big sisters do. Got it?"

"You really think I'm brave?" Apple Bloom asked, smiling.

"Of course I do!" Applejack replied. Apple Bloom considered that for a second.

"Well," she finally said, "then just stop bein' so amazing all the time, and I won't have to work so hard to keep up."

Applejack burst out laughing and hugged her sister tightly. "I'll get right to work on that. But listen up." She looked at Scootaloo and Sweetie Belle, including them in what she said. "One thing my friends and I never do is run and go *lookin'* for danger. I have a feelin' y'all are gonna have plenty of adventures that are gonna give us all kinds of panic attacks. But don't go makin' trouble when you don't need to. Y'all shoulda told us about this bogle."

"We're sorry," Sweetie Belle said.

"But we *were* pretty awesome," Scootaloo added.

"I have no doubt," Applejack said, grinning, "and if I'm bein' honest, I'm pretty impressed. Y'all are gonna have to tell me all about this bogle."

A shriek ripped through the morning air, causing everypony to freeze.

"What in Equestria happened to my fabrics?!" Rarity screamed from her boutique.

Sweetie Belle slowly turned to the others. "We are in *so* much trouble."

EPILOGUE

The Pony once again looked out the window at the expansive Everfree Forest. Not with excitement this time but with concern. The Pony opened the *Book of Legends* and flipped through the pages. Things The Pony had been certain of seemed less so now. There were questions where there hadn't been before. The events of the past couple of days had changed things drastically.

The Pony would have to be patient. Plans would have to wait. The bogle had caused too much attention. And then there was the issue of the three little ponies with the matching cutie marks. That required further investigation. That was unexpected. There was too much at stake here to leave anything to chance. If The Pony's plan was going to succeed, something would have to be done about the Cutie Mark Crusaders.

Tail of the Timberwolf

PROLOGUE

The moon was almost full. Though these "Cutie Mark Crusaders" and their families were proving to be an unexpected complication, The Pony kept focus on the final goal. The Livewood grew far in the distance, in a dark, shadowy patch. It was here, in the heart of the Everfree Forest, where the Artifact would be. How The Pony longed for it! Such power. Such magic!

The Artifact would be fiercely protected. Without a plan to charm the guardians of the Livewood, nopony could set hoof there. Perhaps, with the right encouragement, the guardians could be made to serve The Pony. The only way to know would be to perform a little experiment....

CHAPTER ONE

"Its huge fangs were this close to my face! I could feel its horrible, raspy breath as it got closer. And closer! *Hhhhhuuh haaaaa. Hhhhhuuuh haaaaa!*" Scootaloo breathed noisily, hooves raised like claws as she stalked toward the gathered classmates in the schoolyard.

"However did you escape?" asked Pip, enthralled.

Scootaloo struck her best Rainbow Dash–cool pose. "No monster is a match for *my* wheels! I zoomed circles around that bogle! It would have eaten most of Ponyville if I hadn't chased it back into the Forest and told it to never come back—or else!"

"Uh, Scootaloo? Aren't ya forgettin' somethin'?" Apple Bloom prompted.

Scootaloo blushed. "Apple Bloom, Sweetie Belle, and Lilymoon helped, too," she added.

"And got into lots of trouble for it." Sweetie Belle sighed, remembering the whole terrifying thing. The bogle, a huge, invisible creature, had moved into Miss Cheerilee's Schoolhouse after Lilymoon, the newest student there, accidentally disturbed its nest. Against their sisters' wishes, Apple Bloom and Sweetie Belle teamed up with Scootaloo to lure the bogle back to the Everfree Forest where it belonged. With Lilymoon's help, they decorated the creature's old home with Rarity's beautiful fabric. The bogle loved it!

Most of Ponyville was impressed that

the Cutie Mark Crusaders—Sweetie Belle, Scootaloo, and Apple Bloom—had saved the town from the frightening bogle. But Rarity remained upset. "Couldn't you have used *last* season's fabrics?" Rarity had moaned to her little sister. At least their classmates thought they were heroes.

"If I ever thee another monthster," said Twist, "I'll know which ponieth to call!"

Apple Bloom scuffed a hoof on the ground and sighed in disappointment. "Maybe not. Looks like our first adventure's gonna be our last one for a while. Applejack told me not to take on any more monsters without askin' first."

"Fine by me," Sweetie Belle said. "I don't need an adventure like *that* ever again."

"That's 'cause you're a scaredy-pony," piped up Snips.

Sweetie Belle frowned at him and stomped her hoof. "I am not! I'm just as brave as any—*AAHHH!*" Sweetie Belle shot straight up, startled. Something freezing cold had touched her shoulder! She whirled to see Snails behind her, holding an ice cube with his magic. He chuckled and hoof-bumped Snips.

"You were saying?" Snips laughed. Sweetie Belle glared at the troublemakers, but before she could do anything else, Miss Cheerilee popped her head through the Schoolhouse door.

"Time for class, everypony!" she sang out. As the ponies trotted into the Schoolhouse, Sweetie Belle saw that Lilymoon was already there. She must have arrived early to avoid talking to the other ponies. Besides the CMCs, Lilymoon hadn't made too many friends yet. The violet-eyed Unicorn sat at her desk, staring straight ahead, not making eye contact with anypony.

Diamond Tiara stepped in a wide arc to dramatically avoid Lilymoon's desk. "Careful, Silver Spoon. Creepiness is catching." Diamond Tiara sneered.

Lilymoon shot them an icy look. But she gave a small smile when Sweetie Belle, Apple Bloom, and Scootaloo sat next to her. Miss Cheerilee stood in the front of the classroom, getting everypony's attention.

"Class, I hope you're excited, because Lilymoon has a special surprise for us today!"

The students all shared worried looks. Another surprise from Lilymoon was the last thing they wanted!

CHAPTER TWO

"Do you think it's another bogle?" Featherweight whispered anxiously to Pip. Miss Cheerilee nodded toward Lilymoon, who placed a large bag on her desk and glared out at the class.

"I...made treats for everypony," she said awkwardly. She glanced toward the CMCs, who gave her encouraging nods. Sweetie Belle and her friends had told Lilymoon that sharing sweets was a great way to show the class she was friendly. Sweetie Belle realized they should have told Lilymoon to smile, too. Based on everypony's reaction, the glaring didn't seem to be helping.

"Isn't that nice? Let me go get plates."

Miss Cheerilee smiled, stepping outside. The students eyed Lilymoon.

"What kind of treaths?" Twist asked suspiciously. Lilymoon emptied the bag, revealing a tray of bright-green squares.

"*Ew!* What are they, frog cakes?" Diamond Tiara said, making a face.

"No!" Lilymoon protested. "They're cactus bars!"

"That doesn't sound much better," Silver Spoon said.

"You *eat* cactus?" Snails gaped.

"That'th gross," Twist said, trotting over to peer closer at the bars.

"They're a family recipe...." Lilymoon tried to explain.

"Now I *really* don't want one." Diamond Tiara sniffed. Lilymoon shot her a nasty look. Hearing a rustling noise, Lilymoon looked down to see Twist nosing around in her treat bag. Twist pulled out a large candy cane.

"I'll take thith inthead," she said, marching back to her desk.

"That's actually part of my lunch," Lilymoon protested, but Twist didn't seem to hear.

Sweetie Belle could see this was not going well. She tried to help. Loudly and enthusiastically, so the rest of the class could hear, she said, "Cactus bars sound really interesting! I'll take one!"

"I'll take two!" Apple Bloom chimed in.

"Yeah!" Scootaloo exclaimed. "They sound even cooler than lemon bars!" But when Miss Cheerilee returned with the plates, the Crusaders were the only ones who tried the green treats.

Sweetie Belle could tell Lilymoon was

upset, even though she let her blue-and-white-striped mane cover her face so nopony could see her expression. It would definitely take a lot of work to make the rest of the class accept the new student. But Sweetie Belle resolved she wouldn't give up until they did. Cutie Mark Crusaders didn't quit!

CHAPTER THREE

Lilymoon was quiet as Sweetie Belle, Apple Bloom, and Scootaloo walked her home. Sweetie Belle could see that Lilymoon was still bothered by how the other students had reacted to her cactus bars. She thought rather than bringing it up, it would be better to talk about something else. "Can you believe Snips said I'm a scaredy-pony?" she asked indignantly.

"Well, you don't really like dangerous adventures," Scootaloo pointed out.

"And yer not a big fan of Nightmare Night," Apple Bloom added. Sweetie Belle couldn't believe her friends weren't taking her side!

"I know you're brave," Lilymoon said. "You're coming to *my* house to hang out."

Sweetie Belle had to admit that Lilymoon's house was more than a little spooky. High on Horseshoe Hill, it was covered in vines, practically melting into the trees around it. The floors creaked, the shutters rattled in the wind, and Sweetie Belle could swear the portraits of the ponies on the walls were watching her when she wasn't looking. Still, friends stuck together, no matter how creepy their houses were. As the ponies approached the front door, Lilymoon's ancient aunt popped out of the front hedge, startling them all. Her eyes were wild, and her tangled gray mane stuck out in every direction.

"Auntie Eclipse . . . what are you

doing?" Lilymoon asked. Sweetie Belle thought she sounded worried about what the answer would be.

"Visiting my star spider friends, dear. They weave such interesting webs during the full moon, don't you think?" Auntie Eclipse held up a hoof with spiders crawling all over it. The Crusaders' eyes went wide, but they nodded politely and edged past Auntie to the front door.

"Sorry," Lilymoon whispered. "Auntie is . . . different."

"That's one word for it," Scootaloo murmured. Lilymoon led the others into her house, but before they could reach the stairs, a voice called.

"Lilymoon! You're finally home." Lilymoon's mother, Lumi Nation, walked in from the next room. She stopped when she noticed the other ponies. Sweetie Belle didn't think she was very happy to see them. "And you've brought…friends," Lumi added with no sound of welcome in her voice.

"They're helping me get caught up at school," Lilymoon said.

"Isn't that nice?" Lumi Nation said, but to Sweetie Belle, it sounded like she thought just the opposite. "Well, don't be too long. You have studying to do. And your father is counting on your help in the greenhouse. There isn't much time before tonight."

"Yes, Mother," Lilymoon said, already cantering up the stairs. The others followed, close on her hooves.

"What's tonight?" Scootaloo asked.

"And what's in the greenhouse?" Sweetie Belle wanted to know.

"And what are you studyin'?" Apple Bloom wondered. But Lilymoon shook her head.

"Upstairs," she said. Once they were safely in Lilymoon's room with the door closed, the Crusaders got some answers. "My dad has all kinds of plant experiments you can do only at night," Lilymoon explained. "And as for studying..." She gestured to a dusty stack of thick magical books piled up on her desk. Sweetie Belle thought they'd fit right in at Twilight's library. "My family is big on magical research."

"On top of your regular homework?" Scootaloo asked in disbelief.

Lilymoon nodded. "Guess cactus bars aren't the only weird things about us," she said with a sigh.

"They were good! And the resta the class woulda realized that if they'd tried 'em," Apple Bloom said.

"They just need to get to know you like we do," Scootaloo said.

"How? Have you seen how those other ponies look at me? They'll never forgive me for that bogle, much less talk to me," Lilymoon said.

Sweetie Belle perked up. She had an idea! "A birthday party!" she announced.

"Uh...it's not my birthday," Lilymoon said, raising an eyebrow.

"Not *yours*. Zipporwhill's!" Sweetie Belle said excitedly. "She's having a huge party tonight, and everypony is welcome! If you come, the whole class will see you playing games and having fun—"

"And realize you're just like us!" Scootaloo chimed in.

"Good thinkin', Sweetie Belle!" Apple Bloom said. The Crusaders high-hooved one another in victory. Lilymoon looked thoughtful, but before she could reply, there was a creaking noise outside her door. They all froze. Lilymoon frowned and flung the door open with her magic.

Her sister, Ambermoon, stood in the doorway!

"Were you spying on us?" Lilymoon asked. Ambermoon looked surprised to be caught but quickly covered it up with a haughty expression.

"You were stealing from me again!" Ambermoon sneered.

"*I was not!*" Lilymoon said, outraged.

"So somepony else keeps taking things from my room?" Ambermoon asked.

"Don't be so dramatic." Lilymoon rolled her eyes. "It was *one* candy cane for my lunch!"

"And my hoof polish and my book on dragon scales and my manebrush?" Ambermoon listed each item as if it were the most valuable treasure ever.

"I was borrowing!" Lilymoon exclaimed.

"Stealing," Ambermoon corrected.

"Better than spying," Lilymoon shot back. Ambermoon glared at her sister.

"You're not going anywhere tonight," she said, changing the subject. "Mother will *never* let you go to a Ponyville party."

"I'm not asking *Mother*," Lilymoon

said, trotting past her sister and into
the hallway. The Crusaders hurried to
follow, but Sweetie Belle looked back
to see that Ambermoon was watching
them go with narrowed eyes. Apparently,
Lilymoon and her sister didn't get along
very well.

Lilymoon led her friends outside to
the greenhouse, a small building behind
the cottage made of smoky green glass.
Sweetie Belle thought it looked like the
shiny shell of an enormous beetle squatting
on the lawn. As they all stepped inside,
Sweetie Belle could see the building was
filled from top to bottom with plants.
Some of them she recognized from
Filly Guides as dangerous. And did some
of them have . . . teeth? Sweetie Belle

huddled closer to Scootaloo and Apple Bloom.

Lilymoon's father, Blue Moon, was at the back of the greenhouse. He wore goggles and a lab coat. He looked up and saw his daughter and the Crusaders. He smiled—a little too widely.

"Well, hello there!" he said through his strange grin. "What can I help you young ponies with?"

"My friends invited me to a party, and I really want to go," Lilymoon said in a rush. "It's tonight. Please say yes!"

"Tonight?" Blue Moon asked. Sweetie Belle recognized the look on his face. It was the same look Rarity had whenever she was about to say no to something. Fortunately, Sweetie Belle knew what to do. She gave Blue Moon her biggest, shiniest eyes.

"Pleeeaaase?" she squeaked. Scootaloo and Apple Bloom added their hopeful faces to Sweetie Belle's. It was too much for Blue Moon.

"All right..." he finally agreed. Lilymoon grinned to her friends. But her face froze when he added, "But only if you take Ambermoon with you."

"Don't worry, Father. I'll keep a close eye on her," Ambermoon said, stepping into the greenhouse. Sweetie Belle couldn't be sure, but she thought that sounded like a threat.

CHAPTER FOUR

Zipporwhill really does *have the best parties,*
Sweetie Belle thought. All of Ponyville
Park shone with light-spangled streamers
and glowing balloons as the sun set.
Three piñatas dangled near a table
laden with every type of candy Sweetie
Belle could name—and even some she
couldn't.

Lilymoon hung back, a little
overwhelmed, as the Crusaders led her
into the park. It looked like everypony
in Equestria had shown up for the
birthday bash. Sweetie Belle spotted
most of Miss Cheerilee's class, including
Snips and Snails, who were staggering
out of the park with goody bags

overstuffed with candy. Sweetie Belle waved at Rarity, who was performing onstage with the Pony Tones. Nearby, colts and fillies laughed as they bounced on a pile of fluffy clouds heaped on the ground. Ambermoon was the only pony who didn't seem like she was having fun.

"I'm getting a cup of punch," she announced. "Hurry up and do your thing. We're leaving soon."

"But y'all just got here!" Apple Bloom objected. Ambermoon ignored her and trotted off.

"My sister always gets weird around the full moon," Lilymoon explained, then added, "well, weird*er*."

"SweetieBelleScootalooAppleBloom!"

an energetic Pegasus in glasses and a tiara called as she zoomed over to greet them.

"Zipporwhill! Happy birthday!" the Crusaders exclaimed in unison.

"I'm so glad you made it to my party! Who is this?" Zipporwhill asked, smiling at Lilymoon. The Unicorn backed up a little, unsure what to do.

"This is Lilymoon," Sweetie Belle said, nudging her nervous friend forward. "She's new to Ponyville."

"Hi," Lilymoon said quietly. She was startled when Zipporwhill threw her hooves around her in a fast hug.

"Welcome to my party! Have fun, okay? Don't forget to get your face painted!" Zipporwhill exclaimed happily, then flew off.

"See? Yer fittin' in already." Apple Bloom smiled at Lilymoon.

"Birthday cake *comin' through!*" a loud voice announced. Sweetie Belle looked over to see Pinkie Pie bouncing through the crowd, pushing a cart with a massive three-tiered rainbow-swirl cake with glitter sprinkles. Next to it was a smaller peanut-butter cake in the shape of a bone. Gummy Snap, also on the cart, opened his jaws to take a bite, but Pinkie stopped him just in time. "Don't be silly, Gummy. *That* cake's not for alligators. It's for Zipporwhill's puppy!"

Gummy licked his eyeball thoughtfully. The CMCs hurried after Pinkie Pie as she bounced through the crowd. Then suddenly, the pink pony looked up at the sky and stopped, frozen in place. Sweetie Belle almost crashed right into her as Gummy slid off the cart.

"Pinkie Pie? Are you okay?" Sweetie Belle asked.

"*Oh my gosh!* Do you see how big the *moon* is?!" Pinkie said, shoving the cake-serving tools into the hooves of the surprised Cutie Mark Crusaders. "Can you take care of the cake for me? I just have to do one *liiiiittle* thing. Okaythanksbye!" And Pinkie zipped off at top speed, leaving a dust cloud.

"Is she always like that?" Lilymoon asked, raising an eyebrow. Scootaloo, Sweetie Belle, and Apple Bloom shared a look.

"Yep. Pretty much. Uh-huh," the Crusaders all responded. They began cutting the cake and passing it out to the other partygoers. Everypony was having a blast until...

"*HELP! HELLLLLP!*" Shouts came from across the park. The Pony Tones stopped singing, and everypony turned to see Snails and Snips come racing into the party. They looked terrified. "It's... after...us!" Snails gasped, trying to catch his breath.

"What? What is after you?" asked Zipporwhill, flying over.

"A monster! We were walking out of the park and it attacked us!" Snips said in a rush.

"It was huge, with claws!" Snails nodded. "And big teeth!"

"A monster? I'm not surprised," Diamond Tiara said loudly. "*She* probably invited it." Diamond Tiara pointed a hoof at Lilymoon. The ponies all turned to look at Lilymoon, who glared back at them.

"It wasn't me!" she said defiantly.

Apple Bloom agreed fiercely. "Yeah! She's been with us the whole time!" The CMCs nodded. Zipporwhill's father stepped forward to speak to Snips and Snails.

"Are you sure you did not just encounter the characters I hired for the party?" he asked, gesturing to several ponies in large puppy and kitty costumes. Snips and Snails shook their heads, looking back at the park entrance.

"No, because they're over there...and the monster is *right there!*"

Sweetie Belle whirled to see that the colts were right. A hulking, dark form stood in the shadows at the park's entrance. It tilted back its fierce head and howled.

"It's a Timberwolf!" Lilymoon shouted.

The Timberwolf charged into the party.

CHAPTER FIVE

Sweetie Belle was frozen in fear as the Timberwolf bounded into the park. Its glowing green eyes burned in the darkness. A putrid stench of earth and rotting logs poured from its mouth with every rasping breath. Its "fur" was made of leaves, and its four legs and body were covered in bark, like a living tree-creature. Snips and Snails were right—it had giant teeth and claws. The birthday party exploded into chaos. Ponies screamed and stampeded out of the park as the beast stalked forward, growling. Zipporwhill's father scooped up his struggling daughter in his hooves and flapped his wings skyward.

"My puppy!" Zipporwhill reached her

hooves toward a small brown dog across the park. The little Pegasus squirmed free of her father's grip and flew to grab her puppy. He licked her muzzle in thanks, then began to bark ferociously at something behind Zipporwhill. She turned slowly, her eyes widening in fear. The monster was stalking toward her, head low, jaws agape.

Sweetie Belle gasped as the creature gave a guttural growl and leaped at the birthday pony. Zipporwhill screamed and ducked, flying under the beast, her tiara skimming its belly. The Timberwolf's fangs sank into the piñata dangling behind her, and it shook it vigorously like a dog. As the papier-mâché ripped, sugary missiles of candy flew everywhere.

"Hide!" Lilymoon said as she shoved

the Cutie Mark Crusaders under the cake cart and dashed into the fray.

Sweetie Belle peeked out from the tablecloth and watched as the Timberwolf bounded atop the table of candy. It threw its head back, devouring the sweets with huge gulps. Once it was finished, it raised its muzzle and sniffed the air. Then, it whipped its head toward the cupcake-decorating station. "Oh no," Sweetie Belle whispered. Diamond Tiara and Silver Spoon were trapped inside the cupcake booth, huddled together in terror.

"Run!" the Cutie Mark Crusaders yelled. But either the ponies didn't hear them or they were too afraid to do anything. The Timberwolf took a flying leap from the now-empty candy table and loped toward the cup-cake booth. Diamond Tiara and Silver Spoon

whimpered as the monster approached, sharp wooden teeth gnashing the air.

Suddenly, a cupcake flew from the station and splattered on the Timberwolf's snout. Then another and another! It licked the frosting off its nose and turned to see who its attacker was. Sweetie Belle couldn't believe it! Lilymoon was facing off against the beast, using her magic to hurl cupcakes as fast as she could.

"Run!" Lilymoon called to Diamond Tiara and Silver Spoon. "I'll hold it off!" The terrified ponies didn't need to be told twice. They cantered away to safety.

"She's running out of cupcakes!" Scootaloo hissed.

"We gotta help her!" Apple Bloom said.

Sweetie Belle gulped as her two friends stuck their heads out from under the cake cart and yelled with all their might: *"HEY, TIMBERWOLF! OVER HERE!"*

The beast whipped its head toward the noise, green eyes ablaze. In two huge leaps, it reached the cake cart. Scootaloo and Apple Bloom quickly ducked back under the tablecloth. Sweetie Belle whimpered as she heard the Timberwolf circle the cart. The CMCs held their breaths.

"It's standing next to us," Scootaloo breathed, eyes wide. Sweetie Belle shuddered as she heard the Timberwolf devour the cake above them in loud, messy bites. Then suddenly, the creature stopped eating.

"Is it gone?" Apple Bloom asked.

With a snuffle, the creature stuck its wooden snout under the tablecloth! The Cutie Mark Crusaders screamed and dove away from it.

Then, a blast of Unicorn magic wrapped a ribbon around the Timberwolf's muzzle, tying a bow. Sweetie Belle looked over to see Rarity galloping to the rescue. Applejack raced in to stand protectively in front of the Crusaders. As the Timberwolf pawed at the bow entangling its jaws, Fluttershy stepped forward to address the beast.

"Excuse me, but you were *not* invited to this party. I think you had better go back to the Everfree Forest where you belong!" Fluttershy said sternly.

"Or we're gonna *make* ya go back," Applejack added fiercely. The Timberwolf growled, but to Sweetie Belle's relief, it turned tail and raced out of the park.

"Are y'all all right?" Applejack asked with concern. Rarity dashed over.

"Oh, Sweetie Belle," she said, scooping

her sister into a hug. "Darling, you must have been so frightened."

"I'm *fine!*" Sweetie Belle said, annoyed that Rarity had basically called her a scaredy-pony in front of all her friends, even though she *was* relieved her sister had appeared.

"We're all okay, thanks to Lilymoon!" Apple Bloom said, nodding toward the young Unicorn. Lilymoon was looking around the party.

"Where's my sister?" she asked. But just then, Ambermoon came rushing over from some nearby booths.

"Let's *go*, Lilymoon," she snapped without so much as looking at anypony else. Lilymoon shrugged to the others and rushed off to join her sour-faced sister.

"Y'all should be gettin' home, too,"

Applejack said. "Rarity, ya mind walkin' 'em back?"

"I'm happy to. Now, everypony, just stick close to me. I shall ensure no creature harms a hair on your manes!" Rarity said, gathering the CMCs close.

But as they left, Sweetie Belle looked back over her shoulder at the wreckage of the party. The Timberwolf had eaten the birthday cake, but oddly, it hadn't touched the bone-shaped dog cake.

"I don't understand," she heard Fluttershy tell Applejack. "Timberwolves never leave the Forest without a good reason. I wonder if it was sick."

Sweetie Belle was wondering something herself—what if that monster came back?

CHAPTER SIX

The next day in the schoolyard, everypony was talking about the Timberwolf.

"Did you see its teeth?" Featherweight asked.

"Did you smell its breath?" Peachy Pie countered.

"That was the scariest birthday party ever," said Cotton Cloudy.

Twist listened with wide eyes and sighed. "I wath tho bummed I was thick and didn't get to go, but I gueth I thould be glad I mithed it!"

Sweetie Belle, Scootaloo, and Apple Bloom hung back with Lilymoon. They did not feel like reliving last night's adventure.

"Good thing we saw that monster first

and warned you all," Snips bragged to the class. "We basically saved everypony's life."

But Diamond Tiara was having none of it. "You didn't do anything except run away." She sniffed. Then she turned to scan the playground, eyes narrowed. "Where's Lilymoon?"

"Here we go again," Scootaloo muttered. Sweetie Belle got ready to defend Lilymoon. But Diamond Tiara surprised them all.

"*She's* the real hero!" she said, smiling at Lilymoon. "She chased that horrible thing away from Silver Spoon and me."

"Probably scared it away 'cause she's so weird," Snips said. Snails laughed. Diamond Tiara whirled on the Unicorns.

"You think defending me from creepy tree-creatures is weird?" she demanded.

"We should all thank Lilymoon. We're lucky she's in our class." Diamond Tiara put her hoof around the new pony.

Lilymoon looked uncomfortable. "Apple Bloom and Scootaloo saved *me* from the Timberwolf, too," she muttered.

"What did you do?" Silver Spoon asked.

"Aw, it was nuthin'." Apple Bloom said.

"The best part was when the Timberwolf almost ate us!" Scootaloo said, cutting off her friend. The class leaned in, excited to hear what happened next. Only Sweetie Belle stood back from the group. She felt horrible. She'd just hidden under the cart and hoped she'd stay safe. Lilymoon, Apple Bloom, and Scootaloo had all been so brave.

Maybe Snips was right. Maybe she *was* a scaredy-pony.

CHAPTER SEVEN

Sweetie Belle was troubled for the rest of the day. It seemed like everypony was braver than she was. Nopony could say that she hadn't had her fair share of exciting adventures. But even her closest friends went out of their way to point out that she was the pony who always freaked out first. It was still on her mind when she went to bed that night. So when she was jolted awake by the sound of a mournful howl, she tried to convince herself it was just her overactive imagination. A second, closer howl convinced her it was real. Sweetie Belle ducked under the covers, barely breathing. She heard shouting and running hoofbeats. Something was happening outside. Something scary.

Sweetie Belle wanted to stay there, with the covers over her head, until morning. But she heard her friends' voices in her head, calling her a scaredy-pony. Very slowly, she slid out of bed and moved to the window. Taking a deep breath, she forced herself to look outside.

Rarity was cantering down the street, toward Applejack and Twilight Sparkle, who stood outside Sugarcube Corner. In the light of the full moon, Sweetie Belle could see that the sweet shop's front window had been smashed! Sweetie Belle was still scared, but her curiosity was stronger. She ran downstairs and stepped outside. She started down the street, but two shadowy figures stepped out from a nearby alley. Sweetie Belle screamed... and so did the shadows! As they stepped into the light, Sweetie Belle realized it was Apple Bloom and Scootaloo.

"Don't sneak up on us like that!" Scootaloo said.

"Me? You're the ones hiding in the dark in the middle of the night!" Sweetie Belle protested. Then she added, "Um, why are you hiding in the dark in the middle of the night?"

"The Timberwolf is back!" Apple Bloom blurted. "It attacked Sugarcube Corner!" Sweetie Belle's eyes went wide.

"But it's gone now, right?" she asked, looking around nervously.

"Yep. Mrs. Cake told Applejack what

happened, and she rounded up the others. They all headed over to investigate, so we tagged along," Apple Bloom explained.

"Why didn't you come get *me*?" Sweetie Belle frowned, feeling left out.

"We...didn't want to wake you up!" Scootaloo said. Sweetie Belle looked at her friends suspiciously.

"And...we thought you'd be scared," Scootaloo admitted.

Sweetie Belle *was* scared. But she didn't want to admit it. "I'm a Cutie Mark Crusader! Where you go, I go!" she said. Scootaloo and Apple Bloom smiled and high-hooved Sweetie Belle. Then they galloped down the street to the sweet shop. When they got there, Mrs. Cake was already telling Twilight, Applejack, and Rarity her tale, while Mr. Cake tried to rock the babies, Pumpkin and Pound, back to sleep.

"...And when I came downstairs, there was the monster, eating my éclairs! I didn't think; I just grabbed my rolling pin and chased it away!" Mrs. Cake said.

Sweetie Belle peered around the wreckage of Sugarcube Corner. Half-eaten pastries sagged in the display case, and the normally candy-packed shelves were stripped bare. Even the cake-decorating sugar sprinkles were gone. Her hoof touched something sticky, and she looked down. She had stepped on a caramel apple with massive canine bite marks in it. Sweetie Belle kicked the confection off her hoof and shuddered.

Rainbow Dash flew in, with Fluttershy a wingbeat behind. "We checked everywhere in town!" Rainbow Dash reported. "No sign of the Timberwolf. And those things are pretty hard to hide!"

"I've never heard of a lone Timberwolf attacking a shop before," Twilight said thoughtfully. "Every book I've read says they usually run in packs and prefer the deep forest."

Pinkie Pie bounded down the stairs, yawning. She stopped in her tracks when she saw the huge crowd gathered.

"What's everypony doing here?" she asked brightly. "Is it a surprise party? Who are we surprising? Is it me?" Then she put her hooves over her mouth in concern. "Did I just ruin the surprise part?" she whispered loudly. "I promise I won't tell myself!"

"No, Pinkie," Twilight said, "Sugarcube Corner was attacked by a

Timberwolf. You mean you didn't hear any of it?"

"I'm a heavy sleeper," Pinkie said with a shrug. To demonstrate, she immediately fell asleep standing up, mouth open in a loud snore.

"Pinkie Pie!" Applejack shouted. Pinkie jumped awake again.

"What's everypony doing here?" she asked, smiling brightly. "I just had the *straaaangest* dream that you were throwing me a surprise party!"   .

"I think we should look for clues!" Apple Bloom said, getting things back on track.

"We have to find that Timberwolf before it strikes again!" Scootaloo said.

"Yeah!" Sweetie Belle added, trying to sound like she meant it.

"You three aren't doin' anything. This

is grown-up pony business," Applejack informed the CMCs. "You listenin', Apple Bloom?" she added for good measure.

"Yes," Apple Bloom said sulkily. "But we'd be a big help—"

"I know you would, sugarcube," said Applejack, smiling at her little sister fondly. "But the best thing you can do for us right now is stay safe."

Sweetie Belle gave the tiniest sigh of relief. Staying safe was *definitely* something she could do.

"Actually," said Twilight, "I think I *do* have a job for you three." Apple Bloom and Scootaloo brightened. Sweetie Belle winced. "You can help Mr. and Mrs. Cake clean up their shop!"

Apple Bloom and Scootaloo sagged. Sweetie Belle beamed.

"Meanwhile, the rest of us will try to find that Timberwolf and stop it from attacking again. Maybe Starlight Glimmer and I can find a spell to help." Twilight trotted off to find Starlight.

As Sweetie Belle looked at the fang marks in the caramel apple, she was glad to leave the Timberwolf hunting to Twilight. Still, she felt like maybe she was noticing a pattern to the monster's attacks. And if she was right...she was giving up sugar forever.

"This meeting of the Cutie Mark Crusaders has been called to try 'n' figure out what that Timberwolf is up to!" Apple Bloom announced.

Lilymoon looked from Apple Bloom to Scootaloo and Sweetie Belle. "Does it matter that I'm not a Cutie Mark Crusader?" she asked.

They shook their heads. With all the craziness going on (which they were specifically told *not* to get involved in), Apple Bloom suggested they meet at the Crusaders Clubhouse. At the very least they could try to come up with some ideas to help out their sisters and the others.

"First item on the list," Apple Bloom

read from her notes, "what makes Timberwolves attack?"

"Somepony insulted them?" Scootaloo suggested.

"Their forest home was destroyed?" Lilymoon offered.

"Their bark is worse than their bite?" Scootaloo said, grinning.

"Revenge?" Lilymoon asked.

"Good! What else?" Apple Bloom jotted notes down on a big piece of paper. Sweetie Belle had an idea, but it sounded pretty crazy, even to her... and she was the one who had thought of it! Apple Bloom turned to look at her. "You haven't said anythin' yet, Sweetie Belle. Don'tcha have any ideas?" Sweetie Belle took a deep breath, then launched into her theory in a rush.

"I think the Timberwolf isn't attacking ponies. It's going after sugar! Like at Zipporwhill's birthday party: It ate all the candy on the table. And it went after cupcakes. And it ate the birthday cake, which was sweet, but not the dog cake, which wasn't! And then, it attacked the sugariest part of Ponyville, Mrs. Cake's shop. But it didn't touch anything but the candy and sweets!" Sweetie Belle stopped talking. The others stared at her.

Finally, Apple Bloom sighed. "If you don't have a serious suggestion, you don't need to make stuff up," she said.

"But I *am* being serious!" Sweetie Belle said, her voice cracking indignantly.

"Who ever heard of a Timberwolf eating candy? That's not what those big teeth are for," Scootaloo said.

"Actually," Lilymoon said thoughtfully, "Sweetie Belle might be onto something."

"What?" Scootaloo blurted.

"Ha!" Sweetie Belle said.

"Have you ever heard of wereponies?" Lilymoon asked the others. "Ponies who change into different creatures?"

"There was that one time Fluttershy turned into a vampire fruit bat-pony..." Apple Bloom said, remembering.

"Like that." Lilymoon nodded. "Only it happens on a full moon."

"You think the Timberwolf may be actually...a pony?" Scootaloo asked, her eyes wide.

"Which pony?" Sweetie Belle asked nervously. She knew it couldn't be her friends or her sister, since they had all been around when the monster showed up. But what if it was somepony else she knew, like Mayor Mare? Or Miss Cheerilee!

"I don't know." Lilymoon shrugged. "I'm just saying, this Timberwolf isn't acting like a real Timberwolf. Especially when it comes to candy. But if it was really a werepony who had a sweet tooth..."

"Well, how do you spot a werepony?" Apple Bloom asked.

"I don't know," Lilymoon admitted again. "But I know where we can find out!"

CHAPTER NINE

"I'm *sure* there's a chapter on wereponies in *The Lost Creatures of Equestria*," Lilymoon said as they walked up Horseshoe Hill.

"Didn't we tell our sisters we weren't gonna get into any more monster trouble?" Sweetie Belle asked.

"We aren't gettin' into trouble," Apple Bloom said. "We're just gatherin' information."

Sweetie Belle had a feeling "gathering information" would quickly turn into "getting into trouble." But she didn't want them to think she was scared, so she let it go.

As they reached Lilymoon's house, the front door flew open, and Ambermoon came trotting out. She saw them and rolled her eyes. "Don't you three have your *own* homes to go to?" she asked.

"Sure. But if we didn't come visit, nopony would be around to tell you that you'd be a lot happier if you weren't so nasty all the time," Scootaloo shot back. Ambermoon's eyes widened in surprise.

"Where are you going?" Lilymoon asked quickly, changing the subject.

Ambermoon continued glaring at Scootaloo but answered her sister's question. "Well, since *somepony* in this house keeps stealing my candy, I'm going into town to get some more."

"*Ugh!*" Lilymoon groaned. "I'll never borrow *anything* from you *ever* again, happy?"

"Happi*er*," Ambermoon said as she trotted down the hill.

"So?" Apple Bloom asked casually. "Has your sister *always* liked candy?"

"Yeah...she's had a sweet tooth for as long as I can..." Lilymoon's eyes widened. "But...it couldn't be her! She was at the party with us!"

"She *did* kinda disappear right before the Timberwolf showed up, though," Apple Bloom pointed out.

"And you *did* say she acts weirder during a full moon," Sweetie Belle reminded her.

"I *totally* bet it's her!" Scootaloo said. "*That's* why she's so mean."

"She's *always* that mean." Lilymoon shrugged. "It doesn't mean she's a werepony."

"Wereponies?" Somepony cackled above them. They all looked up to see

Auntie Eclipse trotting down the stairs. "Now, why would such innocent little fillies be talking about wereponies?"

Sweetie Belle glanced nervously at the others. Should they tell Auntie Eclipse what they thought was going on? Lilymoon subtly shook her head. Sweetie Belle sighed. Of course they weren't gonna do that.

"We just…uh…have a report for class," Apple Bloom lied.

"Everypony got different creatures," Scootaloo added. "We got a werepony! So we were just gonna check out a book in your library to see what it said about ponies and Timberwolves and—"

"Timberwolves?" Auntie Eclipse interrupted her. "You want to know about ponies turning into Timberwolves!" The ponies nodded. "Timberwolves aren't like regular wolves."

"Duh," Scootaloo said. "They're made of timber." Auntie Eclipse arched an eyebrow at Scootaloo. "Sorry," she said quickly.

"It's a rare magic that brings wood to life. In fact, it's only ever been found in one place in all of Equestria."

"The Everfree Forest?" Lilymoon asked.

Auntie Eclipse nodded. "Timberwolves have never been spotted anywhere else. And you won't find any books about ponies turning into Timberwolves because it's not possible. Not the same way they would turn into a werepony. Seems like a strange assignment to give young fillies...." Auntie Eclipse let the comment hang in the air. The young ponies all glanced at one another, unsure of what to say next.

"Thanks for your help," Apple Bloom finally said. "I'm sure we can find the rest of what we need on our own." She started toward the library.

"Actually," Auntie Eclipse said, stepping in front of her, "I'll be needing the library this afternoon. I'm sure you have more than enough information...for a school project." She strode into the library, the door magically closing behind her.

"Wow," Scootaloo said. "Guess she really doesn't want us in there."

"Great," Lilymoon said. "Where are we gonna get answers now?"

"*Actually*," Apple Bloom said with a grin, "there may be *some*pony who could help us...."

CHAPTER TEN

Sweetie Belle shuddered at the spooky trees and strange sounds of creatures that stayed *just* out of sight. For somepony who didn't like scary places, she sure found herself in the Everfree Forest a whole lot. Fortunately, she knew where they were going, and that place didn't scare her at all...anymore. Still, Sweetie Belle didn't want to spend any more time in the spooky forest than she absolutely had to.

"You know a Zebra? And she lives *in* the Everfree Forest?" Lilymoon asked as they walked along the path. "You think she'll help us?"

"Zecora helped me when I got Cutie Pox," Apple Bloom said. "I betcha she

knows about curing other curses, too."
They turned a corner and saw a hooded
figure gathering plants just off the path.
The figure turned and regarded the fillies.

"Four ponies where there are usually
three—have you all come out here just to
see me?" The figure removed her hood, and
Zecora smiled at them.

"Hi, Zecora!" the Crusaders said in
unison.

Zecora glanced at Lilymoon. "I'm
always happy to have guests. Who might
you be? I know the rest."

"H-hi," Lilymoon said shyly, "I'm
Lilymoon. My family just moved here."

Zecora nodded, then turned and
walked along the path. "Follow me and
sit a spell. I'm sure you all have much to

tell," she said over her shoulder. The others quickly followed.

Sweetie Belle heard Lilymoon gasp when they arrived at Zecora's home. It *was* pretty impressive. Zecora lived inside a giant tree. Different-colored bottles filled with Celestia-knew-what dangled from the branches outside. Sweetie Belle looked around as they walked through the door. A cauldron was bubbling, odd objects hung on the walls, and the shelves were filled with spells and potions. Zecora checked the bubbling cauldron as she regarded the young ponies.

"I sense this is more than a friendly visit? You all look worried; so come now, what is it?"

"We know it sounds crazy, but we

think the Timberwolf that attacked Ponyville is really a werepony," Apple Bloom explained.

Zecora's eyes widened. "A werepony can bring much danger. But a werepony Timberwolf? That's even stranger."

"Very strange," Lilymoon agreed. "My aunt told us a werepony Timberwolf was impossible."

"I don't want to say that your aunt was wrong, but it *is* possible, if the magic is strong." Lilymoon looked surprised that her aunt might not be right about something. Zecora cocked her head. "But I'm confused. Please explain to me: Why would a Timberwolf be a pony?"

Scootaloo nodded to Sweetie Belle, who was getting way more comfortable in Zecora's familiar home than out in the Forest. "I noticed that both times this Timberwolf attacked, it only ate candy," Sweetie Belle said. "Which seemed really weird."

"Yes, I see," said Zecora, "that is quite suspicious. You think it's somepony who finds candy delicious." The ponies nodded. "A spell this strong is very impressive. But the pony who cast it is clearly aggressive."

"I didn't even think about that," Apple Bloom admitted. "Who would turn a pony into a Timberwolf?"

"*Why* would someone turn a pony into a Timberwolf?" Scootaloo added.

Zecora looked away from the ponies. She stared out the window into the Forest beyond. Sweetie Belle thought she looked...worried? "I have an idea, but I don't want to say. I believe that's a tale to tell some other day. For now, let's just focus on getting a cure. We will know more when it's time, I am sure."

Zecora wandered around the room as she spoke, gathering bottles, herbs, and various ingredients. She tossed them into the boiling cauldron. "To avoid serious trouble, there is no time to waste. You must locate the pony and do it with haste!"

"You mean so it won't have time to attack again?" asked Scootaloo.

Zecora shook her head. "There are bigger things at play than you understand. If you don't cure this pony as fast as you can, it may never turn back to a pony again!" The fillies all looked at one another.

"It becomes permanent?" Sweetie Belle squeaked. Zecora nodded.

"But how are we going to figure out who it is?" Lilymoon asked.

"Maybe we already have," Scootaloo said.

"It's *not* my sister," Lilymoon insisted.

Zecora took an empty bottle and filled it with the milky-gray potion bubbling in her cauldron. "A Timberwolf pony could hide anywhere. But when you do find it, you must pluck a hair."

"We have to *what?*" Sweetie Belle asked.

Zecora handed Apple Bloom the bottle filled with potion. "Put the hair in the potion and watch it turn pink; when the pony turns Timberwolf, give it this drink."

"Are we sure we want to do this?" Sweetie Belle hesitated.

But Apple Bloom's enthusiasm overpowered the sentiment. "Wow. Thanks,

Zecora! I knew you'd know what to do!" she said, studying the potion. She turned to the others. "Come on, y'all! We got no time to waste!"

The ponies all rushed toward the door— Sweetie Belle with less speed than the others—but Zecora's voice stopped them: "One final thing: When the suspect you find, here is a warning to keep in your mind." The ponies all stopped and turned. Zecora looked at them with a very serious expression. "Don't let it scratch you, whatever you do, or else you will turn into a Timberwolf, too!"

"Did you hear her? *We* could become Timberwolves!" Sweetie Belle called, rushing after the others as they hurried toward Ponyville. Apple Bloom, Scootaloo, and Lilymoon were busy discussing what to do next.

"How do we get the Timberwolf to drink the potion?" Scootaloo asked.

"We know it likes candy. We could pour it on something sweet!" Lilymoon suggested.

Sweetie Belle couldn't believe what she was hearing. "We aren't gonna do anything!" she said loudly. Everypony turned to look at her. "Our sisters *told* us not to get into trouble, remember?" The others stopped running and considered what she said.

Apple Bloom sighed heavily. "Sweetie Belle is right, y'all," she said. "We *did* promise not to get into more mischief."

"Thank you!" Sweetie Belle was relieved.

"But everypony still thinks it's a regular Timberwolf!" Scootaloo said. "We need to tell them it's really Ambermoon!"

"We don't *know* my sister is a werepony!" Lilymoon reminded them. She thought for a minute, then: "It could be one of your sisters' friends."

"What? Who?" Apple Bloom asked.

"The pink one. Pinkie Pie? She was acting pretty strange at the party," Lilymoon pointed out.

"Yeah, but that's Pinkie. She *always* acts weird," Apple Bloom said.

"She *did* say she slept through the whole Timberwolf attack," Sweetie Belle realized. "That does seem a little suspicious."

"You just don't want Ambermoon to be the werepony, so you're trying to make us think it's Pinkie!" Scootaloo accused Lilymoon. The Unicorn rolled her eyes.

"You just don't like my sister, so you want her to be a werepony," she huffed.

Scootaloo considered that. "Okay, that's actually kind of true," she admitted.

"If we tell Rarity and her friends what we know," Sweetie Belle said, "they can check out Pinkie *and* Ambermoon."

"We should get a hair from Ambermoon's mane or tail," Apple Bloom said. "Just in case."

"Actually..." Lilymoon reached into her bag and pulled out a manebrush. "The hair

is no problem. I still haven't returned this."
She magically pulled a long black hair from
the brush. She looked at the others. "If my
sister *is* the werepony, we can handle it."

"And if it's Pinkie . . . either way, we
gotta tell the others right now!" Apple
Bloom decided. "Let's hustle, y'all!"

They raced back to Ponyville. The
sun was setting when they arrived, but
the town was bustling. They quickly
realized why. Rarity, Applejack, and
their friends were preparing to head off
into the Everfree Forest to hunt down the
Timberwolf! The CMCs had arrived just
in time! They rushed through the crowd.

"Rarity!" Sweetie Belle called. Rarity
turned and saw the fillies approaching.

"Sweetie Belle, darling, we're just a teensy
bit busy at the moment," Rarity explained.

"Perhaps whatever it is can wait until after we've dealt with this beastly business?"

"We're here because of the beastly business!" Apple Bloom explained.

"Oh *no*, you ain't," Applejack said, walking over to them. "If I told you once, I told you a dozen times: *We* are handlin' this!"

"We *know*!" Apple Bloom said. "But we need to tell you *what* you're handling!"

"Don't worry," Fluttershy said sweetly as she walked past them. "We know just how to take care of the poor creature."

"You do?" Scootaloo asked.

"Sure," Applejack said. "We're gonna find it, catch it, and take it far away where it can't harm nopony."

"You can't!" Sweetie Belle squeaked. "It's not a regular Timberwolf! It's a—"

"We doin' this or what?" Rainbow Dash called out to the others.

"One second!" Applejack called back, then turned to the fillies. "We appreciate y'all wantin' to help. But we do this stuff all the time."

"Don't worry about us," Rarity said to Sweetie Belle reassuringly.

"Rarity. We aren't worried. But you don't—"

"Pinkie, dear, are you quite all right?" asked Rarity, cutting off her sister. Sweetie Belle and the others turned and saw Pinkie Pie walking toward them, strangely subdued.

"Never better," Pinkie said. She really didn't look so good, but she was putting on a brave face for the task at hand. "Let's do this thing!" She walked past the fillies as she struggled to smile. As she passed, Sweetie Belle saw Lilymoon use magic to pluck a hair from Pinkie's tail. Nopony else noticed, and Pinkie didn't even flinch! As they trotted off, Applejack and Rarity glanced back at the fillies.

"Y'all go home. Stay outta trouble," Applejack warned.

"Don't be scared, Sweetie Belle. We shall be fine!" Rarity called. The grown-up ponies all hurried into the Forest, Twilight leading the way.

"I can't believe it," Scootaloo said.

"They wouldn't even listen to us!" Apple Bloom said, kicking her hoof in the dirt angrily. "If we're right, they're gonna take some poor pony and dump it Celestia-knows-where!"

"If it is my sister . . . she'll be stuck as a

Timberwolf forever." Lilymoon looked horrified.

"And if it *is* Pinkie," Scootaloo said, looking at the rising dusk, "and she transforms into a werepony when she's with the others..." They all looked up at the sky. The full moon would be out soon. Sweetie Belle was the one who finally said what they were all thinking, even though she didn't want to.

"We have to go find the Timberwolf first, don't we?"

CHAPTER TWELVE

"Are we sure this is the best plan?"
Sweetie Belle asked as she walked over
to the others. They were standing by
the entrance to the Everfree Forest. She
adjusted the knapsack on her back. They
each wore one filled with candy. They had
raided their emergency Nightmare Night
supplies to make sure they had enough for
the mission.

"We don't have a choice. We only got
one shot at this," Apple Bloom said. She
pulled Zecora's potion out of her bag. "We
go in, find the Timberwolf, and get it to
drink this here potion!"

"Well, first, we have to figure out who
the Timberwolf is," Lilymoon reminded

them. She opened her bag, one black hair and one pink hair visible inside. "Once we find out which one it is, we drop the hair in the potion..."

"And wait for it to turn pink," Scootaloo finished. She reached into her bag and pulled out a buckball-size peppermint. "Once it does, we pour the potion on this. We know that whoever it is likes candy. *This* they won't be able to pass up!"

Sweetie Belle was terrified, but she was determined to do what needed to be done. A pony's life was at stake! Maybe Ambermoon, maybe Pinkie Pie. She would *not* be a scaredy-pony.

"You ready?" Apple Bloom asked. Sweetie Belle screamed and jumped.

"Yes. Sorry. I–I'm just a little nervous,"

Sweetie Belle replied. The others looked at one another.

"Sweetie Belle, nopony will be upset if you don't come," Apple Bloom said gently.

Sweetie Belle took a deep breath. She could do this. "We have a pony to save! Let's go, Crusaders."

Apple Bloom smiled. They all hoof-bumped and marched into the Everfree Forest as the last rays of sunlight faded on the horizon.

Continuing deeper into the Forest, they left a trail of candy behind them. Whoever the Timberwolf was, the sugar would be too much to resist. After they had been at it a while, Sweetie Belle was starting to wonder if the plan was going to work at all.

Then she heard a noise.

"What was that?" Sweetie Belle asked nervously. The others stopped and listened, but there was nothing but the sounds of the Forest.

"It's just your imagination," Scootaloo said. But a second later, it happened again. This time Lilymoon heard it, too.

"It sounds like...paper?" Lilymoon said. The ponies all quietly made their way through the Forest, following the noise. Above them, clouds blanketed the night sky, blocking the moonlight and making it hard to see. However, they could *hear* the rustling noise getting louder. Scootaloo motioned to the others and pointed toward a ravine up ahead. The fillies all crept closer. They poked their heads over a ridge and looked down to see what was making the noise. A shadowy figure was hunched over a large mound of something.

"Is that... *Twist*?" Sweetie Belle whispered. Below them in the ravine, Twist sat next to a pile of candy. The rustling they had heard was her unwrapping the candy before she popped in into her mouth.

"She took all our candy!" Scootaloo said. "Now the werepony will never get it!"

"Twist! Cut it out!" Apple Bloom yelled, jumping over the ridge. Twist looked up, shocked to see them.

"What are you guyth doing out here?!" she asked nervously.

"We are *tryin'* to find a werepony. But you're eatin' all our bait!" Apple Bloom shouted.

Twist looked scared. But why would she be scared of them?

"Pleath! You all have to go!" Twist said. "Before ith too late!"

"Too late for what?" Scootaloo asked. Above them, the clouds parted, and the light of the full moon shone down on the ravine. Twist doubled over, like she had a really bad stomachache.

"You guys..." Lilymoon said, backing away slowly. Tiny leaves popped out of Twist's mane. Vines wrapped around her hooves.

"Oh no..." Scootaloo said.

"Hey. It's okay, Twist," Apple Bloom said slowly as she motioned for them all to back out of the ravine. "Why don't you keep the candy?"

Twist howled up at the moon. The fillies turned and rushed out of the ravine.

But Lilymoon suddenly stopped. She looked back at Twist.

"Hang on!" she called. She rushed down as Twist continued her transformation.

"Lilymoon! Be careful!" Sweetie Belle yelled.

Lilymoon leaped down next to Twist. Leaves, wood, and moss covered her body, but her orange tail was still visible. Lilymoon snagged a single hair in her teeth and rushed back to join the others. As they hurried out of the ravine, Sweetie Belle glanced back down. The transformation was complete.

They had found the werepony. Twist was the Timberwolf!

CHAPTER THIRTEEN

The Timberwolf snarled and stuck her wooden muzzle to snuffle at the pile of empty wrappers. There was no candy left. She sniffed the air. Her head turned, and her glowing eyes stared right at the ponies. Sweetie Belle couldn't move. Glancing to either side, she could see that for once, she wasn't the only one frozen with fear. Next to her, Scootaloo, Apple Bloom, and Lilymoon stood just as still.

Twist growled and took a few steps toward them.

"The candy. In the bags," Lilymoon whispered.

"Should we leave the candy and run?" Scootaloo asked.

"We need to get the potion ready," Apple Bloom whispered back.

"We need to get away!" Sweetie Belle said. "We can't help Twist if we're Timberwolf chow."

"I thought you said this Timberwolf only ate sweets," Scootaloo whispered.

"*You* wanna be the one to test that?" Sweetie Belle hissed.

Below them, the Timberwolf moved cautiously but steadily closer.

"Here." Lilymoon's horn glowed brightly, and the hair from Twist's tail floated over to Sweetie Belle. "You go get the potion ready while the Timberwolf is distracted."

Lilymoon charged down the ravine toward the Timberwolf. Her horn glowed, and the knapsack on her back flew into the air, just in front of Twist's wooden nose.

"Hungry?" Lilymoon shouted. Twist growled at Lilymoon but didn't take her eyes off the floating bag of candy. She swiped at it with a massive paw.

"Wow. Lilymoon is awesome," Apple Bloom said breathlessly.

"Yeah. That's brave right there," Scootaloo agreed. Sweetie Belle nodded. She could never do anything like that.

Lilymoon yelled up at them. "This is going to be a pretty lame diversion if there's nothing to *divert from*!"

"Oh. Right!" Apple Bloom grabbed the potion and pulled out the stopper. Sweetie Belle's horn glowed, and Twist's hair floated into the liquid. The Crusaders watched as the liquid began to bubble and swirl from milky gray to bright pink.

"*Oooh*. Pretty," Sweetie Belle whispered. The other two stared at her. "What?" she said. "It *is*!"

Scootaloo dug the giant peppermint out of her bag and poured the pink potion over it. The elixir soaked into the candy, and it glowed brightly.

"Um. *Hey, guys!*" Lilymoon called after them. They turned and saw her up in the branches of a tree on the opposite ridge of the ravine. Twist clawed the tree with her front paws.

"Okay, Crusaders. Let's do this!" Apple Bloom and Scootaloo rushed down the ravine. As scared as she was, Sweetie Belle was just behind them.

"Don't let her scratch you!" she reminded her friends.

The Timberwolf turned when she heard them rushing toward her.

"Mmm," Scootaloo said, holding the glowing peppermint in front of her. "Doesn't this look nice and tasty, Twist?" The Timberwolf licked the bark around her mouth with her leafy tongue. She took a few steps toward them. Sweetie Belle smiled—it was going to work! They were going to save Twist!

Suddenly, a rope lassoed the Timberwolf's mouth shut and pulled her away from the peppermint! Sweetie Belle looked at the top of the ridge and saw Applejack, Rarity, and the others. Applejack held the rope and glared down at the fillies.

"Y'all step *away* from that Timberwolf."

CHAPTER FOURTEEN

"Wait!" Sweetie Belle squeaked, but nopony was listening. Twilight Sparkle blasted a beam of purple light from her horn, encasing the entire ravine in a magical shield.

"Ravine is secure," she called to the others. "Now let's get that Timberwolf and transport it out of here."

"You can't do that!" Lilymoon called from the tree.

"Oh, we can, and we totally will," Rainbow Dash said confidently as she hovered in the air. The Timberwolf leaped and tried to claw at Rainbow Dash, but Applejack tugged on the rope, jerking away the Timberwolf's muzzle.

Applejack ignored its growls and glared at her sister.

"Y'all got some serious explaining to do!" she said.

"We *will* explain, if y'all will just stop and listen for a second!" Apple Bloom replied. Rarity and Pinkie Pie slid down into the ravine and blocked the Timberwolf on either side.

"*After* you fillies are out of danger," Rarity said firmly as Fluttershy cautiously approached the Timberwolf.

"Hello there. You must be scared. How about you let us help you?" she said sweetly. The Timberwolf tried backing away from Fluttershy, but Applejack held her securely with the rope.

"Just let us feed her this peppermint,

and *then* it will all make sense!" demanded Scootaloo.

"Timberwolves don't eat peppermints, silly!" Pinkie Pie said, giggling.

"*This* one does!" Lilymoon said, leaping in front of Fluttershy. "Show them," she said to Scootaloo, using her magic to untie Applejack's lasso.

"Hey now! Stop that!" demanded Applejack. As soon as the Timberwolf was freed, she roared and tried to run away. But Twilight's shield prevented her from going anywhere.

"Here!" Scootaloo shouted as she rushed toward the Timberwolf with the peppermint.

"Whoa, whoa, whoa! What are you thinking?" Rainbow Dash said as she swooped down and grabbed Scootaloo. "That thing is dangerous!"

"No!" Scootaloo shouted as the peppermint flew out of her hooves and landed in the dirt below, right next to Sweetie Belle, who picked it up.

"Toss it here, Sweetie Belle!" Apple Bloom called.

"Sweetie Belle, you put that down this instant!" Rarity shouted.

The Timberwolf crouched defensively, her back against Twilight's shield.

"Oh for Cerberus's sake," Lilymoon said, running toward Sweetie Belle and the peppermint, "none of you are listening! Sweetie Belle, throw it to me!"

Pinkie bounced over and hugged Lilymoon tightly, then asked, "Hey, what gives, sister? Are you on Team Pony or Team Timberwolf here?"

The Timberwolf was ready to leap at anypony who came close. Applejack rushed toward it. The Timberwolf slashed at her with her claws. Sweetie Belle gasped! At the last moment, Applejack ducked, and the wooden claws harmlessly raked against her hat.

"A little scratch ain't gonna bother me none, fella," Applejack said, looking for an opening.

"*Sis!*" Apple Bloom ran and barreled into her older sister, knocking her out of the way just as the Timberwolf slashed at her again. "Stay back! If she scratches you, you'll turn into a Timberwolf, too!"

"Say what, now?" Applejack asked as she stood up.

"Twist is a werepony," Lilymoon explained.

"Twist? That's *Twist*?" Pinkie Pie asked.

"That's what we've been *trying to tell you*!" Scootaloo called from above, still in Rainbow Dash's hooves. Everypony started talking at once.

The Timberwolf turned in a snarling circle, confused by all the shouting. Sweetie Belle stared at the peppermint in her hooves. Looking around, she saw that everypony was busy yelling. She really wished she could explain it all and not have to be the brave one, but so far that had been a disaster. This *had* to be done—now. Sweetie Belle took a big breath. She didn't think about it. She just ran as fast as she could toward Twist.

"Sweetie Belle! No!" Rarity called. But Sweetie Belle kept going. The Timberwolf turned toward her and roared out a fog of sour green breath.

"Not a scaredy-pony. Not a scaredy-pony. Not a scaredy-pony," Sweetie Belle whispered to herself over and over again. Just a few more feet. She was almost there. Everypony shouted as Sweetie Belle jumped into the air. The Timberwolf leaped to meet her, its jaws gaping wide... and Sweetie Belle jammed the peppermint into the Timberwolf's wide mouth.

The Timberwolf collapsed, as if she had suddenly fallen into a deep sleep. Rarity rushed toward Sweetie Belle and helped her up.

"Sweetie Belle, what were you thinking?" she asked.

"Somepony had to help Twist," Sweetie Belle said shakily. Twilight's shield vanished, and she trotted over to join them.

"Now, what is all this about a werepony?" Twilight asked.

"It's a long story," Lilymoon stated. "But the short version is, Sweetie Belle figured out the Timberwolf was a werepony, we got a cure from Zecora, and then—"

"We *tried* to tell y'all so you could handle it. But you were so busy protectin' us, you wouldn't listen," Apple Bloom finished, glaring at her sister.

"So we had to deal with it ourselves," Scootaloo explained. "We thought the Timberwolf was either Lilymoon's sister or Pinkie Pie."

"Why me?" Pinkie Pie asked, shocked.

"You were acting really weird at Zipporwhill's party," Apple Bloom said, "and you said you slept through the Timberwolf attack on Sugarcube Corner."

"*Ohhhhhh.* Well, that's because I was trying to break the Equestria record for Earth pony unicycle juggling on the first night of a full moon. See?" Pinkie whipped three unicycles out of nowhere and began juggling them as the others gaped. "It made me kinda tired the next day."

"Anyhow … we came out here because we were worried about you guys," Scootaloo continued. "And then we found out the Timberwolf was Twist. But we couldn't let you send her away, or she'd get stuck as a werepony forever!"

"Wow," Twilight said. "That's … really good work."

"Definitely," Rainbow Dash added. "You guys were pretty awesome. *Especially* standing up to us!"

"Hey now," Applejack said as Rarity sniffed. "Don't push it."

Behind them, somepony groaned. A pile of wood, leaves, and bark lay where the Timberwolf had been. Twist poked out her head. She looked around, confused.

"Hey, you guyth. Whath goin' on?" she asked. Lilymoon and the Crusaders rushed over to her.

"Twist, are you okay?" Sweetie Belle asked.

"I think tho," she responded.

"What happened?" asked Apple Bloom.

"I hafth *no* idea," Twist said as she crawled out of the pile. "I got home from thchool the other day and felt groth. Tho I thtayed home from the party. But then... I had a crathy dream... and I wanted to eat loth and loth of candy... I thaw thom ponies in the Forest, and felt really funny..."

"It wasn't a dream," Lilymoon said seriously. Then she smiled and nodded toward Apple Bloom, Scootaloo, and Sweetie Belle. "But you're okay now. Thanks to the Cutie Mark Crusaders."

Apple Bloom put her hoof around Lilymoon and said, "*All* the Cutie Mark Crusaders." Lilymoon beamed.

"I guess I owe you an apology, sugarcube," Applejack told her sister. "We shoulda listened to y'all."

"It's okay . . . for *now*." Apple Bloom smiled. "But *next* time you'd better listen."

"Next time? I swear, you just love findin' trouble, don'tcha?"

As the Apple sisters continued to bicker, Rarity turned to Sweetie Belle.

"Sweetie Belle, darling, I'm so proud of you," she said.

"*Awwww* . . . I'm just glad I wasn't a scaredy-pony," Sweetie Belle said happily.

"Are you kidding?" Scootaloo said. "After *that* move? *Nopony* can ever call you scared again!"

Twilight was staring up at the moon thoughtfully. She looked at the Crusaders.

"Even though I don't love you putting yourselves in danger, we all owe you our thanks. You did some excellent research. But did you ever figure out *how* Twist became a werepony?" The Crusaders all shook their heads.

"That's the one thing we can't quite get," Apple Bloom admitted. Twilight looked troubled.

"What's wrong, Twilight?" Rainbow Dash asked.

"There's some dangerous magic being cast here in Ponyville. And I don't like it." The Alicorn princess frowned.

"And then, Sweetie Belle galloped past everypony, ran straight at the Timberwolf, *leaped* into the air"—Scootaloo jumped onto the seesaw on the playground for dramatic effect—"and soared across the ravine. The Timberwolf jumped up at her, her sharp claws slashing the air! *Wshh! Wshh!* But Sweetie Belle wasn't having it! She crammed the candy *right* in the monster's slobbering jaws!" Scootaloo turned to Twist. "No offense."

"It'th fine!" Twist said, grinning. "Thath totally what happened! Thweetie Belle thaved my life!" The other ponies on the playground all turned to look at

Sweetie Belle, who was standing off to the side, blushing.

"*That* Sweetie Belle?" Snips asked.

"Are you *sure*?" Snails added.

"It wasn't exactly like that. Everypony helped." Sweetie Belle wanted her friends to get the credit they deserved.

"But you *did* leap into the air and make Twist eat the candy?" Silver Spoon confirmed.

"Um. Yeah." Sweetie Belle's blush intensified. It was nice not being the scaredy-pony anymore, but all the attention made her nervous.

"Weren't you frightened?" Pip wondered.

"How did you figure it all out?" Diamond Tiara looked very impressed.

"Lilymoon did. She's the one who

guessed the Timberwolf was really a werepony," Sweetie Belle explained. The other ponies turned and looked at Lilymoon, who smiled shyly.

"Well," Diamond Tiara announced, "between that and saving our lives at the party, I just don't know *how* we managed to survive in Ponyville without you!" The ponies gathered around Lilymoon, asking her what other cool and mysterious things she knew about. As she answered, she glanced over to the Cutie Mark Crusaders and smiled gratefully. Apple Bloom, Sweetie Belle, and Scootaloo all watched her proudly.

"Looks like Lilymoon is finally settling in," Scootaloo observed. "Guess it's a happy ending for everypony."

"*Mmm-hm!*" Sweetie Belle agreed.

"Rarity *finally* forgave me for the fabric we took for the bogle. She said next time we go monster hunting, just check with her first."

"Yeah, Applejack feels awful about almost sendin' Twist away," Apple Bloom said, grinning. "She promised to listen to us about stuff like this from now on. And you know my sister never lies."

Twist joined the Crusaders. "Thankth again, you guyth. Thorry if I thcared you when I wath a Timberwolf."

"We're just glad you're okay," Apple Bloom said.

"Well, not *totally* okay," Twist said, frowning. "The thought of thomething thweet maketh me thick now. The latht *normal* pieth of candy I ate wath that candy cane I got from Lilymoon." She ran off to join the other ponies, and Scootaloo looked at the others.

"That's the candy cane that came from Ambermoon's room! And right after eating it, Twist got so sick she had to miss Zipporwhill's party."

"Only she didn't," Apple Bloom added. "She showed up as a Timberwolf!"

"You think the candy cane turned her into a werepony?" Sweetie Belle asked. "That's crazy!"

"Well, we used a peppermint to cure her," Apple Bloom pointed out. "Is it any weirder that a candy cane started this whole thing?"

"So I was *almost* right!" Scootaloo said triumphantly. "Ambermoon wasn't the werepony, but she's the one who *turned* Twist into a werepony!"

"Maybe," Apple Bloom said, working through it in her head. "But nopony expected Twist to eat that candy. So it's not like Ambermoon did it on purpose."

"Still," Sweetie Belle wondered, "why would Ambermoon have a candy cane that could turn a pony into a Timberwolf?" They all looked over at Lilymoon, who seemed to actually be enjoying herself with the rest of the class.

"She's finally fitting in and now *this* happens?" Sweetie Belle sighed.

"Let's keep it to ourselves for now," Apple Bloom said.

"Because you don't wanna tell her that her sister is evil?" asked Scootaloo.

"No," Apple Bloom said. "I wanna wait until we know if she's in on it or not."

Although things hadn't gone exactly as The Pony had planned, the experiment had still proven useful. It seemed that a Timberwolf was difficult to control, even if there was a pony inside. Using a werepony to get past the Timberwolf guardians wasn't the way to reach the Livewood. If The Pony wanted the Artifact, another plan was needed.

But first, The Pony would have to deal with the Cutie Mark Crusaders. The Pony had gone back to study the scrolls. They were clear that the Artifact would be activated by "the matching marks three." The Pony had thought there was only one group with such marks. But apparently, that wasn't the case.

Fortunately, those meddling ponies had made a habit of coming up to the house on Horseshoe Hill. It wouldn't be a problem to arrange for a little "accident" sometime soon to make sure they didn't cause any more trouble.

Riddle of
the Rusty
Horseshoe

The Pony moved through the Everfree Forest, making no noise at all, almost as if they were part of the shadows themselves. They passed the ridiculously cheerful nest of the bogle and groaned in disgust. Thanks to those annoyingly resourceful Cutie Mark Crusaders, the bogle now had a taste for bright, pretty fabrics and shiny objects. How embarrassing! The Pony slipped past the Poison Joke Tree and traveled deeper into the darkness, finally arriving at their intended destination.

The Pony stood at the edge of a clearing. This was as close as they could get to the Livewood. No amount of magic would keep the twisting vines and branches from noticing them. Just then, a deep growl caught The Pony's attention. Four Timberwolves glared at The Pony from beyond the writhing trees. The Livewood was their home, and what The Pony desired was theirs to guard.

The Pony could feel the magic pouring out of the Livewood and shivered with the need to find a way in. The Pony knew what was inside, just waiting to be taken. But first The Pony had to find a way to keep the Cutie Mark Crusaders from getting any closer to the secrets that would lead them here.

"Be careful!" Sweetie Belle called to Scootaloo. "If you fall, the lava is going to burn you to a crisp!"

"I can't make it!" Scootaloo said, looking down nervously.

"You got this, Scootaloo!" Apple Bloom said. Scootaloo stared ahead at the giant chasm. Apple Bloom and Sweetie Belle stood anxiously on the other side. She took a deep breath and leaped toward them! Wings flapping frantically, she sailed through the air...but not far enough.

"No!" Scootaloo called, reaching out with a hoof as she fell to her doom.

"I don't get it," Lilymoon said, standing off to the side watching the life-or-death struggle unfold in front of her. Apple Bloom and Sweetie Belle stood on top of the bookcase in Lilymoon's bedroom. Scootaloo was on the ground between the bed and the bookcase in the throes of agony. She stopped writhing and looked over at Lilymoon, rolling her eyes.

"What's to get?" Scootaloo asked, hopping up. "The floor is lava. Anything that's not the floor is safe. If you touch the floor, you're out."

Lilymoon looked dubiously at the Crusaders. "And this is really what other fillies do at sleepovers?" she asked.

"Yeah. The good ones, anyway," Scootaloo said confidently.

"I still don't get it," Lilymoon said again.

"It's just *fun*!" Scootaloo said. "You know, fun? That thing ponies do when they aren't being attacked by crazy monsters?" When it came to battling a bogle or tracking a Timberwolf, Lilymoon was definitely the kind of pony you wanted on your side. But Scootaloo was realizing that when it came to simply hanging out, Lilymoon had a lot to learn.

"Well, this is your house and your first sleepover," Apple Bloom interjected as she hopped down off the bookcase. "What do you want to do?" When Lilymoon had casually admitted she had never had friends over for a sleepover, Apple Bloom said they had to plan one right away. Between the creepy house and Lilymoon's strange family, Scootaloo wasn't sure spending the night here would have been her first choice for a relaxing evening, but Apple Bloom had insisted.

"I really don't know *what* we should do," Lilymoon admitted after considering for a few seconds.

"Well," Apple Bloom said, "we could play board games, do arts and crafts, tell ghost stories. Whatever we want!" Lately, Apple Bloom and Lilymoon had been spending a *lot* of time together. Scootaloo felt like Apple Bloom had made it her personal mission to show Lilymoon what fun and friendship was all about. And of course, Scootaloo knew Apple Bloom meant well. But she couldn't help noticing that the more focused Apple Bloom was on Lilymoon, the less attention she gave Scootaloo and Sweetie Belle.

"Well, I *do* like spooky things," Lilymoon stated. "I bet I could tell some good ghost stories!"

"Great!" Apple Bloom said. "The spookier, the better!" Scootaloo glanced at Sweetie Belle, who looked less than excited at the prospect of spooky stories told in the bedroom of an already-scary house.

"Is that okay with you, Sweetie Belle?" Scootaloo asked.

"Why wouldn't it be okay with her?" Apple Bloom challenged. Sweetie Belle looked back and forth between her two friends.

"It's fine. Ghost stories sound great." Sweetie Belle was trying to act excited, but Scootaloo knew that even though Sweetie Belle had been very brave as of late, particularly when they were hunting the Timberwolf, she still wasn't the type of pony who liked getting scared for fun. Of course, that was something Apple Bloom would have thought about as well, if she weren't so focused on making sure Lilymoon was having the perfect sleepover.

"Okay, y'all. Let's set the mood," Apple Bloom said as she turned the lights down in the room.

"You sure you're okay with this?" Scootaloo whispered to Sweetie Belle.

"I'll be fine," Sweetie Belle whispered back. "You don't think Lilymoon's story will be that scary, do you?" They both looked over at Lilymoon, who stared at them ominously, her piercing violet eyes shining brightly.

"The story I'm about to tell you is the most terrifying tale I ever heard—" Lilymoon whispered. Sweetie Belle groaned quietly next to Scootaloo.

"Hey, maybe I should go first!"

Scootaloo interrupted. At least she could make sure her story wasn't too scary. In fact, she could tell a ghost story Sweetie Belle already knew! She grabbed a blanket and pulled it around her like a shawl. "The tale of the *Olden Pony*! It was a night *just* like this one—"

"Hey now! Lilymoon wanted to tell her story!" Apple Bloom said, annoyed. "Besides, that story ain't scary. We've *heard* it!"

"*Lilymoon* hasn't heard it," Scootaloo shot back.

"I don't have to go first," Lilymoon said nervously. She was clearly uncomfortable with the arguing. "Who is this Olden Pony?"

"She's older than *anypony* you've ever seen," Scootaloo said. "And she's looking for her rusty horseshoe."

"That's not how the story starts!" Apple Bloom groaned. "*First* there's the young ponies on a date—"

"It's *my* story," Scootaloo said.

"*Your* story? Why? 'Cause it gave you nightmares the first time you heard it?" Apple Bloom shot back. Scootaloo gaped at Apple Bloom. She couldn't believe she had just said that! Nopony aside from the Crusaders and Rainbow Dash knew how much that story had scared her, and Apple Bloom had just blurted it out in front of Lilymoon!

"Maybe we should play a game? Oubliettes and Ogres?" Sweetie Belle said, trying to calm things down.

"You all can do whatever you want to do," Scootaloo said, dropping the "shawl" and walking toward the bedroom door. "I'm going downstairs. I…need a snack."

"Should we all do that?" Lilymoon asked.

"No," Scootaloo said firmly. "I'm fine by myself." Scootaloo hurried out of the room, slamming the door behind her.

CHAPTER TWO

Scootaloo stormed down the dark hallway. She, Sweetie Belle, and Apple Bloom had been best friends for as long as she could remember. The three of them had been through so much together. But ever since Lilymoon and her family had shown up, things seemed to be changing, and Scootaloo didn't like it. It wasn't that she didn't like Lilymoon. If anything, life in Ponyville had been more interesting than ever since Lilymoon's family moved into the house on Horseshoe Hill. But things between Apple Bloom and Scootaloo were different now, and she wasn't sure what to do about it.

Scootaloo jumped as something

creaked in the shadows. She might like Lilymoon, but she didn't feel the same about Lilymoon's house. It always felt like somepony was watching you. Scootaloo looked at the framed pictures on the wall as she walked down the hall. There were no photos of Lilymoon and her sister, Ambermoon, as little fillies, no fun family vacation pictures. Instead, there were photos of strange creatures Scootaloo had never heard of hanging next to maps and old newspaper clippings. It looked more like a museum than a home.

Something creaked again. Closer this time.

"Hello?" Scootaloo whispered. But nopony answered. She rolled her eyes. "Come on, Scootaloo. It's just your imagination," she muttered to herself.

She made her way down the stairs to the first floor. Something howled in the distance outside. Scootaloo trotted over to a window and stared out at the backyard. The house on Horseshoe Hill was closer to the Everfree Forest than any other house in Ponyville. In fact, technically it was *in* the forest, although just barely. Behind the house stood the shadowy hulk of Lilymoon's family's greenhouse, and beyond *that* stretched the dark wilds of the Everfree Forest. Scootaloo gulped as she studied the backyard. Who knew what kinds of creatures were lurking just outside the window? Creatures looking to make a late-night snack of a small pony who was herself looking for a late-night snack....

"What are you doing?" a voice whispered in her ear.

"AHHHHHPLEASEDONTEATME!"
Scootaloo yelled. Startled, she ran as fast
as she could, right out the back door. She
wasn't paying attention to where she was
going; she just wanted to get away from
whatever was behind her. However, she
quickly realized that there could be
something just as dangerous *outside* the
house, which meant she wasn't any safer
than she had been. Moonlight glinting off
smoky green glass caught her eye.

Scootaloo changed direction and
rushed toward the shelter of the
greenhouse. Once inside, she hurried past
the reaching leaves and tangled stems of
the strange flora toward the back of the
greenhouse to find a good hiding spot, and
glanced behind her to see if she was being
followed. She didn't see anypony…or any

other creature. But just as Scootaloo turned to face forward again, she slammed into a huge ceramic pot and fell backward. The pot—and the large feathery plant inside it—wobbled. She reached out to keep it from tipping, but it was too late. The pot crashed over, pouring dirt and the feathery plant onto the floor.

"Scootaloo?" an annoyed voice shouted. "Why are you in my dad's greenhouse in the middle of the night?"

Scootaloo knew that voice. It was Ambermoon, Lilymoon's sister. She and Scootaloo did *not* get along.

CHAPTER THREE

"What do you think you're doing out here?" Ambermoon called from the front of the greenhouse.

Scootaloo looked at the fallen plant. Great! *Another* reason for Ambermoon to get snotty with her. She quickly set the pot upright and scooped a few hoof-fuls of dirt back into it before grabbing the feathery plant and jamming it into the pot. Just then, Ambermoon trotted around a large purple cactus and spotted her. She glared at Scootaloo. So Scootaloo glared back.

"What are you up to?" Ambermoon asked suspiciously. "And why did you run out of the house when I tried to talk to you?"

"You mean when you tried to scare me?" Scootaloo responded angrily. Ambermoon rolled her eyes.

"I just wanted to know why you were sneaking around my house in the middle of the night!" Ambermoon shot back.

"I wasn't *sneaking*. I was going to get a snack," Scootaloo explained.

"So you steal our food, snoop around our house, and don't actually sleep. Is that how a sleepover works?" Ambermoon glanced at the greenery next to her. "Should I make sure you didn't take any plants while you were at it?"

"With an attitude like that, it's no wonder you don't know what happens at a sleepover. Who would want to hang out with you?" Scootaloo trotted past

Ambermoon. "Now, if you'll excuse me, I'm going to the kitchen."

"Me too. To make sure you don't go poking around anywhere else you're not invited."

"Whatever." Scootaloo huffed. They both walked back into the house. Scootaloo studied Ambermoon out of the corner of her eye as they went. It wasn't just that Scootaloo didn't really like her; she also didn't trust her. The Crusaders were pretty sure that Ambermoon was responsible for their recent Timberwolf trouble. At the Schoolhouse, Twist had taken a candy cane from Lilymoon's lunch bag. When she ate it, the candy cane transformed Twist into a werepony! The Crusaders and Lilymoon had to get a spell from Zecora to cure her. Later, they found out that the candy cane had come from Ambermoon's room. Scootaloo could think of a few reasons somepony might have a candy cane that could turn another pony into a monster, and none of them were good. But the Crusaders wanted to wait for more proof before they told Lilymoon their suspicions. Until then, they had agreed to keep an eye out for anything else that seemed odd. Like Ambermoon sneaking around in the middle of the night...

"So," Scootaloo said casually as they entered the kitchen, "why are *you* awake?"

Ambermoon studied the kitchen counter as she answered. "My room is right next to Lilymoon's. You four were keeping me up with all your carrying on."

"Oh," Scootaloo said. They probably

had been pretty loud. "How much did you hear?" Without looking up, Ambermoon arched an eyebrow.

"Enough to know that this 'snack break' is just an excuse to get away from your friends for a while."

Great! So she knew Scootaloo was mad at Apple Bloom. Ambermoon was the *last* pony Scootaloo wanted in her business!

"It's no big deal," Scootaloo said quickly.

"Of course not." Ambermoon sounded annoyed. "You felt left out for the first time in your life. Did you expect me to give you a pep talk?"

"So you just came out here to rub it in?" Scootaloo demanded.

"No!" Ambermoon was quiet for a minute, weighing her options, then she finally said, "I...was just making sure you were okay." Scootaloo was speechless. Why would Ambermoon, who had never been anything but mean to her, care if she was okay?

"Where is it?" a strange voice whispered.

"What was that?" Scootaloo said, looking around the room.

"I said I wanted to make sure you were okay," Ambermoon repeated.

"Not that. The other thing!" Scootaloo ran past Ambermoon and looked down the dark hallway.

"What other thing?" Ambermoon looked around, confused.

"WHERE IS IT?" The voice was raspy. And it was getting louder.

"That!" Scootaloo rushed out of the kitchen toward the foyer, following the noise. It sounded like something she had

heard once before in a dream. But it couldn't be…

"Hey! Wait up!" Ambermoon called after her.

Scootaloo rushed into the foyer and gasped. There, at the top of the stairs, slowly walking toward her, was the Olden Pony from her ghost story! But this was no ghost story; this was a very real pony. And she walked slowly down the very real stairs, muttering to herself in a terrifying low growl.

The Olden Pony looked just like Scootaloo remembered from her nightmares. She was ancient, with knobby knees and flea-bitten flanks. She wore a tattered shawl that was hundreds of moons old. Wisps of white mane stuck out from her bun. Two long hairs grew out of a mole on her wrinkled chin. One red eye squinted shut while the other glowed bright blue. And it was glaring straight at Scootaloo.

She couldn't believe it. The Olden Pony was real.

"Where is my rusty horseshoe?" the Olden Pony moaned.

Scootaloo panicked. She desperately dashed for the front door, shoving past Ambermoon, who had just entered the foyer.

"Scootaloo! Why are you acting so weird?" Scootaloo heard Ambermoon call after her. But she couldn't stop. Her hooves wouldn't let her. She just had to get away from the Olden Pony. She had to get home.

CHAPTER FOUR

The next morning, when Scootaloo opened her eyes and found herself in her own bed, she briefly thought everything had been a dream. She hopped up and headed toward the kitchen. But when she rushed into the hallway, she heard a curdling scream.

"Oh! For Celestia's sake!" an Earth pony exclaimed, picking up the basket of laundry she'd just dropped. "What are you doing here, Scootaloo? I thought you were spending the night up at your new friend's house?" So it hadn't been a dream. Scootaloo *had* gotten in a fight with Apple Bloom and run into a creature right out of her nightmares. Awesome.

"Hey, Aunt Holiday," Scootaloo said sullenly. "I...wasn't feeling good so I came home." Aunt Holiday studied Scootaloo with concern, clearly not buying it. But she didn't pry; Aunt Holiday always let Scootaloo tell her things when she was ready.

"Well, head on into the kitchen. Auntie Lofty's already in there. I'll make you some breakfast in just a second."

Scootaloo nodded and went into the kitchen, where a sturdy Pegasus, Auntie Lofty, was scarfing down a plate of eggs. She looked up at Scootaloo, surprised.

"Hey, slugger! What are you doing here?" Auntie Lofty asked.

"I came home last night! It's not a big deal!" Scootaloo said more forcefully than she intended. Lofty arched an eyebrow. In contrast to Aunt Holiday, *she* never let things rest until she had answers. Aunt Holiday came trotting into the room and kissed Lofty on top of her head.

"Let me make Scootaloo some breakfast first, dear. *Then* you can give her the third degree." Scootaloo sighed. Aunt Holiday was her dad's older sister. Recently, she and Auntie Lofty had started staying with Scootaloo when her parents were away, which was most of the time. Unlike her parents, they were *always* interested in what was going on in her life. Usually it was nice that they cared, but this morning, she wished they would just leave things be. Scootaloo sat down at the kitchen table, where Auntie Lofty eyed her suspiciously. A knock at the door rescued Scootaloo from Lofty's gaze.

"I'll get it!" Scootaloo said, jumping up and rushing to the door. She opened it to find Apple Bloom, Sweetie Belle, Lilymoon, *and* Ambermoon standing there. They all looked at her with varying degrees of worry.

"Oh. Hey, guys," Scootaloo said, not quite sure what to say.

"Hey," Apple Bloom said, equally as uncomfortable. "We just wanted to make sure you were okay. Ambermoon told us you left in a hurry last night." Scootaloo looked at Ambermoon. Why hadn't she told them about the spooky, old pony on the stairs?

"Well, of course I did…I saw the Olden Pony coming down the stairs toward me. What else was I gonna do?" The fillies all glanced at one another, confused.

Ambermoon looked back at Scootaloo. "There wasn't anypony on the stairs. We were in the kitchen, then you ran into the foyer and out of the house," she explained.

"What? No. I saw her!" Scootaloo insisted. "She was right there on the stairs! She was asking about her rusty horseshoe!" Scootaloo couldn't believe Ambermoon was lying!

"Well," Apple Bloom began, "maybe you just thought you saw the Olden Pony after I reminded you of how scared you used to be of her." She looked like she wanted to say more, but Scootaloo didn't give her a chance.

"Can you *please* stop bringing that up?!" Scootaloo said angrily. "I don't need you telling everypony else what a scaredy-pony you think I am!"

"That ain't what I'm sayin'!" Apple Bloom responded.

"You're just saying you don't believe me," Scootaloo said.

"Well, if Ambermoon didn't see anything—" Sweetie Belle began.

"Oh, so *now* you trust Ambermoon?" Scootaloo asked.

"What does *that* mean?" Ambermoon said, looking at the others.

"Nothin'," Apple Bloom said. She turned to Scootaloo. "Okay, so you think you saw something last night."

"I *did* see something last night. The Olden Pony," Scootaloo stated.

"But isn't that just a ghost story?" Lilymoon asked. Scootaloo's wings fluttered in annoyance.

"Look," she said, "I *know* it's a ghost story. I *know* she's not supposed to be real. But I also know what I saw. It *was* her. She

was there. I don't know how, but she was."
She looked at the others. She could tell
they were at a loss for what to say. They
really didn't believe her. She was just going
to have to find a way to prove to them it
was true!

"Thanks for coming by to check on
me," Scootaloo said, then forced a fake
yawn and stretched her hooves. "I think
maybe I just need some rest. I'll catch up
with you later."

"You sure?" Sweetie Belle asked. "We
thought maybe we could all go over to
Sugarcube Corner and—"

"It's okay," Scootaloo said quickly, "I'm
not that hungry. Have fun!" She went
back inside, leaving her confused friends to
stare at one another quizzically on the
doorstep.

CHAPTER FIVE

After a hearty breakfast spent avoiding answering Auntie Lofty's questions, Scootaloo headed into town. If she was going to prove that the Olden Pony was real, she needed more information. For that, she knew *just* who to talk to. Scootaloo felt a little bit better now that she had a plan. She just wished she didn't have to do it alone. She was used to having her friends by her side.

"Doesn't look like you're getting much rest," somepony said. Scootaloo turned. Ambermoon was leaning against a tree. Scootaloo huffed and kept walking. Ambermoon rushed over to walk alongside her.

"You sure seem to like following me,"

Scootaloo said. "Planning to spy some more and then lie to my friends that I'm seeing things?"

"I didn't say you were seeing things. I just said *I* didn't see anything. Because I didn't," Ambermoon explained. "But after talking to you this morning, I realized something must have happened—I just wasn't sure what. And that's what I told your friends." Scootaloo still couldn't believe Ambermoon hadn't seen anything, but there was nopony else around, so she had no reason to lie.

"Yeah? Where are they now?" Scootaloo asked, pretending to be disinterested.

"Sugarcube Corner. Although they all looked pretty bummed to go without you." Scootaloo felt better knowing her friends missed her. If only they believed her, too.

"Why did you stick around?" Scootaloo asked, honestly curious. Ambermoon stared straight ahead, not making eye contact.

"I could tell you were planning something. And I saw how scared you were last night. I felt bad. So I...wanted to help if I could." Scootaloo stopped walking and stared at Ambermoon.

"Okay, *hold* on. Last night you said you wanted to check on me. Now you want to help me. We don't even like each other! Why are you doing this?"

"I can see how much Lilymoon likes hanging out with all of you," Ambermoon explained. "She seems...happier since she met you. It made me think...it might be nice to have a friend. So I'm trying to be friendly." Ambermoon looked at Scootaloo and forced a wide smile. The weird grin had the opposite effect Ambermoon was going for, but she seemed to be sincere. Maybe she wasn't as bad as Scootaloo had thought she was. Scootaloo still didn't completely trust her, but...it was nice having somepony on her side. Even if it wasn't the pony she was expecting.

"Okay, fine," Scootaloo said. "You can hang out with me. *For now.* C'mon." She nudged Ambermoon's shoulder to follow.

"Where are we going?" Ambermoon asked.

"To get answers about the Olden Pony story from the most awesome pony in Equestria. The pony who told me the story in the first place: Rainbow Dash."

It took a little time, a lot of asking around, and a ton of side errands, but they finally found Rainbow Dash flying out of

Rarity's boutique. She was carrying her Wonderbolts uniform and was in a hurry.

"Hey! Rainbow Dash!" Scootaloo called, waving at the blue Pegasus. Rainbow Dash saw her and veered over.

"Hey, Scoot. Hey, Scoot's friend. Can't talk long. I'm in a hurry! Gotta get ready to go to Canterlot for the Royal Flyfest! It's gonna be so *awesome*!"

"Oh *wow*! The Flyfest!" Scootaloo exclaimed. "That sounds *amazing*! What tricks are you planning?" Ambermoon cleared her throat, reminding Scootaloo why they were there. "Oh. Right," Scootaloo said. "Hey, before you go, can I ask you something about the Olden Pony?"

"The what now?" Rainbow Dash frowned.

"You know, that spooky story you told me a long time ago." Scootaloo squinted one eye and hobbled toward Rainbow Dash. "'Who has my rusty horseshoe?' Is there any more to it?" Scootaloo asked.

Rainbow Dash shook her head. "Nope. Long time ago. Spooky night. Some ponies walking through the woods; Olden Pony wants her rusty horseshoe. Boom!" Then she added, "I mean, when I tell it, it *feels* like there's more to the story, because I'm a *really* good storyteller." Rainbow Dash glanced around. "Hey, where're Apple Bloom and Sweetie Belle? Aren't you all attached at the flank?"

"Um." Scootaloo kicked a rock with her hoof. "I...don't wanna talk about it."

"Whoa. Whoa." Rainbow Dash landed next to Scootaloo and Ambermoon.

"I may be in a hurry, but I've always got time when something's wrong with a friend. And something is definitely wrong. What's up?"

"Things have just been weird lately," Scootaloo mumbled.

Rainbow Dash nodded. "I see," she said. "Well, I know *just* how to fix that!"

"You do?" Scootaloo asked.

"Yup! Sometimes friendships can go through ups and downs. But doing something awesome together always helps. Go round up the others. You're all gonna be my special guests tomorrow at the Canterlot Royal Flyfest!"

CHAPTER SIX

The rest of the day was a blur of activity. Scootaloo and Ambermoon rushed to Sugarcube Corner to tell the others about the invitation. Despite the weirdness between Scootaloo and Apple Bloom, everypony was beyond excited. A chance to see the Wonderbolts live was never something anypony would pass up!

Ambermoon and Lilymoon ran home to make sure it was okay with their parents that they tag along, while the Crusaders ran to the clubhouse where they had a pile of Rainbow Dash posters ready to go. (Scootaloo always made sure there were GO, RAINBOW DASH! and RAINBOW DASH IS AWESOME! posters for any occasion.)

Nopony brought up what Scootaloo had seen the night before. It still bugged Scootaloo that the others didn't believe her, but until she had proof that what she saw was real, she didn't want to get into another argument with Apple Bloom. Apple Bloom seemed to feel the same way. She kept the conversation focused on the Wonderbolts and how much Lilymoon was going to love watching them fly. Sweetie Belle kept glancing back and forth between Scootaloo and Apple Bloom. She knew things weren't fine, but she didn't seem to know what to do about it, so she just kept smiling and saying, "Yay, Wonderbolts," a lot.

Scootaloo was relieved that she made it through the night without seeing or hearing anything strange, and bright and early the next morning the Crusaders, Lilymoon, and Ambermoon met Rainbow Dash at the train station.

"Come on! Let's go, go, go!" Rainbow Dash said as she hurried them all onto the Friendship Express. "I have to get to Canterlot in time to rehearse!"

"This is so exciting!" Lilymoon said, smiling wider than Scootaloo had ever seen. "I've only ever heard about the Wonderbolts! I can't wait to actually see them!" She sat down next to the window as the train slowly left the station.

"It's gonna be amazin'!" Apple Bloom grinned, sitting down next to her. Sweetie Belle climbed into the seat in front of them. Scootaloo saw that Ambermoon was sitting a bit off to the side by herself. She walked past the open seat next to

Sweetie Belle and sat next to Ambermoon instead. Everypony, including Ambermoon, was surprised.

"I'm glad you could come," Scootaloo said as she settled next to the Unicorn. Ambermoon smiled shyly back.

"Me too," she said. "It took some convincing, but since this is the first thing my sister and I have ever wanted to do together, my parents finally gave in." In front of them, Lilymoon said something and Apple Bloom laughed *loudly*. Scootaloo rolled her eyes, then pointedly laughed even louder.

"Ha-ha-ha! That's hilarious, Ambermoon!" Scootaloo shouted. Apple Bloom, Sweetie Belle, and Lilymoon all turned to look back at them. Ambermoon eyed her strangely.

"What about that was hilarious?" she asked.

"Nothing, I just—" Scootaloo began, but a raspy voice cut her off.

"Where is it?" The voice rose from a growl to a shriek. *"WHERE IS MY RUSTY HORSESHOE?"*

"What was that?" Ambermoon yelped, jumping out of her seat and looking around the train. Scootaloo stared at her.

"You heard it, too?" Scootaloo asked.

"Everypony on the train must have heard that!" Ambermoon replied. They both looked around. Apple Bloom, Lilymoon, and Sweetie Belle were chatting softly. In fact, aside from a few passengers eyeing them curiously, everypony else was sitting quietly.

"That was *her*!" Scootaloo whispered.

"The Olden Pony." Ambermoon looked thoughtful, then glanced around the train.

"Okay. Well, even though I don't see her, I clearly heard her. So it isn't just in your head," she said matter-of-factly.

"I *told* you," Scootaloo replied triumphantly.

"But now we need to figure out what's happening. Let's—"

"Hey, you two!" Sweetie Belle called, waving to them. "Come here for a sec!"

"Maybe she heard it, too!" Scootaloo said, and the two of them joined the others. But Sweetie Belle's happy smile made it clear that this wasn't about anything spooky.

"I just wanted to say I'm really glad Ambermoon and Lilymoon could join us for this trip. Scootaloo *and* Apple Bloom and I are looking forward to *all* of us spending time together." Scootaloo realized what the loud *and* between her name and Apple Bloom's meant. It was about as close as Sweetie Belle was going to get to telling her friends to cut it out and play nice. Scootaloo really wanted to get back to talking to Ambermoon about the Olden Pony, but she appreciated what one of her best friends was trying to do.

"Let's all just have fun today," Sweetie Belle added. "Deal?" she said as she stuck out her hoof. Apple Bloom grinned and did the same.

"Deal," Apple Bloom said.

"Deal," Lilymoon and Ambermoon both said as they stuck their hooves in.

"Deal," Scootaloo said, sticking her hoof in and bumping it with the others.

Maybe Rainbow Dash is right, Scootaloo thought. Maybe all you needed to fix friendship problems was a trip to a Wonderbolts show. Now if only that could solve the Olden Pony problem, too....

CHAPTER SEVEN

"Fillies and gentlecolts! Please put your hooves together forrrrrrrrrrrr the—" The announcer barely got out the word *"Wonderbolts!"* before the crowd went wild! Ponies screamed and cheered as the Wonderbolts soared over the stadium into the arena. Celestia had just lowered the sun, and giant lights pointing skyward illuminated the Pegasi's trademark blue-and-gold uniforms as they streaked across the star-filled night.

The seating for the Canterlot Royal Arena was built into the side of a huge cliff for perfect viewing. Hundreds of ponies filled the stands, stomping their hooves with excitement as a crew of Pegasi shifted cloud and rainbow obstacles into place for the Wonderbolts' daring maneuvers. Usually Scootaloo would have been cheering louder than anypony, but with everything going on, she was having trouble focusing.

"*Wow!*" exclaimed Lilymoon.

"*Go, Rainbow Dash!*" Sweetie Belle and Apple Bloom screamed.

Sweetie Belle nudged Scootaloo. "Hey, you okay?" Scootaloo glanced over at Ambermoon. Before the show had started, Ambermoon suggested they tell the others what they had heard on the train. But Scootaloo had insisted they wait until *after* the Wonderbolts' performance. She knew Rainbow Dash loved nothing more than performing for her friends, and she wanted everypony's focus to be on her hero. The mystery stuff could wait until later.

"I'm fine," she lied. Scootaloo looked up at the Wonderbolts flying in formation. She easily spotted Rainbow Dash and smiled. Rainbow Dash always got annoyed with this part of the performance, because she said she had to fly slower than she wanted in order to keep pace with the others. But despite that, she always managed to fly at exactly the right speed. Rainbow Dash, Soarin', Spitfire, and the others were all perfectly in sync. Scootaloo glanced over at Apple Bloom. She realized that not being perfectly in sync with her best friend was bothering her just as much as the problem with the Olden Pony. Apple Bloom glanced over and saw Scootaloo looking at her. She gave a small smile and waved. Scootaloo smiled back. Maybe everything would be—

The Olden Pony's voice cut through the crowd like a knife. *"WHERE IS MY RUSTY HORSESHOE?"*

Scootaloo could feel Ambermoon tense up beside her. But this time, she saw Apple Bloom, Sweetie Belle, and Lilymoon freeze as well!

"Rusty horseshoe?" Sweetie Belle squeaked.

"You heard that?" Scootaloo asked.

Apple Bloom nodded, her eyes wide.

"Not just heard it…" Lilymoon said, pointing at the stairs below their seats.

The Olden Pony was slowly hobbling toward them, her red eye glaring balefully at them.

"*I know you have it,*" she croaked, pointing at them. "*Give it to me!*"

But this time, Scootaloo was ready. Back when she'd still had nightmares about the Olden Pony, there had been one way to stop her. Scootaloo pulled a rusty horseshoe out of her saddlebag and tossed it toward the ancient mare.

"Take it!" Scootaloo cried. The Olden Pony squinted down at the horseshoe. Then she gave Scootaloo a wicked smile.

"*That's not going to work this time, dearie.*" Scootaloo gasped as the Olden Pony kicked the horseshoe away and kept stalking toward them.

"Everypony, stay calm," Ambermoon said, taking charge. "We don't know what she is, but we know she isn't real. She can't hurt us."

Scootaloo glanced at the ponies behind and around them. They were whispering to one another and starting to look at the CMCs and their friends strangely. It was obvious that none of the other audience members could see the Olden Pony. Scootaloo looked back down to the stairs and gulped. The Olden Pony was gone.

"Not real? Can't hurt you?" Stale breath brushed Scootaloo's neck. Dreading what she'd see but knowing she had to look, she slowly turned. The Olden Pony was standing right next to her! The ancient mare reached out her hoof and shoved Scootaloo's shoulder. Scootaloo stumbled backward.

"She can touch us!" Scootaloo yelled. More ponies in the crowd turned to see what was

going on. The Olden Pony cackled, the sound of dead leaves tossed in a winter gale.

"NOW, WHERE IS IT?" the Olden Pony demanded.

"Run!" Apple Bloom yelled. The fillies all scrambled away from the terrifying ancient mare.

"Hey!"

"Watch it!"

"What are you doing?"

Ponies yelled as the Crusaders and the Moon Sisters pushed through the crowd in a panic.

"Wait!" shouted Ambermoon. "Even if we escape, aren't the rest of these ponies in danger?"

"I don't know," Scootaloo admitted. At that, Ambermoon turned and started running up the stairs, in the opposite direction of the exit.

"Where are you goin'?" Apple Bloom called.

"The stands aren't safe! Somepony needs to stop the show!" Ambermoon yelled back.

"Stop the *show*?" Scootaloo yelped. She looked at Apple Bloom and Sweetie Belle, panicked. "We can't stop the show!"

Apple Bloom pointed at the Olden Pony, who was closing in on them, moving surprisingly fast for her apparent age.

"We got bigger problems right now, don'tcha think?" The fillies rushed to the top of the stadium. Ambermoon burst into the announcer's booth, the others right behind her. The announcer pony turned and looked at them in shock.

"Hey! You ponies can't be in here!" he exclaimed.

"We have to stop the show right now," Ambermoon said firmly.

"What? *Why?*" the pony asked.

"*Yes, why?*" The Olden Pony was suddenly standing behind the announcer. He didn't seem to hear her and just kept staring at the fillies. *"Afraid I'm going to scare everypony? Cause them to panic?"* With a wicked smile, she reached out and pulled a lever. All the lights in the stadium turned off, leaving everypony in total darkness.

"What happened?" the announcer yelled. Outside the booth, ponies starting yelling and screaming in confusion and panic. Scootaloo couldn't see anything. All she could hear was the laughter of the Olden Pony echoing in her ears.

CHAPTER EIGHT

"I don't even know where to begin."
Rainbow Dash flew back and forth as the
Friendship Express chugged steadily
toward Ponyville. Scootaloo, Apple Bloom,
Sweetie Belle, Lilymoon, and Ambermoon
sat sullenly in their seats. "What were you
thinking?"

"We told you—" Scootaloo began, but
Rainbow Dash held up a hoof.

"Do *not* mention the Olden Pony. The
ponies in the stands said you started
screaming for no reason, pushed through
the crowd, ran up to the booth, and told
the announcer to stop the show. Nopony
saw *anything* following you."

"I know it sounds crazy. And at first we

didn't see anything, either, but it really was—"

Rainbow Dash held up her other hoof. "No. Olden. Pony," she said through gritted teeth. She shook her head and looked down at Scootaloo. "I'm just really disappointed in all of you. You were my guests. And you ruined the entire event." She turned to leave. Scootaloo rushed over and grabbed her hoof.

"I'm really sorry, Rainbow Dash," Scootaloo said. Rainbow Dash shook her head sadly.

"Let's just deal with this later. I'm going up to the front of the train. When we're back in Ponyville, we're getting your families together and we're having a serious talk." She flew out of the train cabin.

Scootaloo stared out the window as the

sun began to rise. She had never felt worse in her entire life. Rainbow Dash had *never* been this upset with her. *Ever.* Scootaloo could feel tears welling up in her eyes. The fight with Apple Bloom, the Olden Pony, and now ruining the Wonderbolts' show? It was all too much. She buried her face in her hooves. A second later, she felt a hoof on her shoulder. She looked up and saw that it was Apple Bloom.

"I'm sorry," she said.

"Why? It's not your fault I'm a huge disappointment to the greatest pony of all time," Scootaloo said sadly.

"No. I mean, I'm sorry about that, too. But…I'm sorry I didn't believe you. And I'm sorry I was mean to you the other night. If I hadn't said what I said about you bein' scared of that story, you never woulda gone downstairs, and none of this woulda happened. It's all my fault."

Scootaloo let out a long sigh and hugged Apple Bloom. "It's not your fault, and I'm sorry, too," she said. "If I'm being honest, I was just jealous. You and Lilymoon have been spending so much time together that I was just worried you'd forget *our* friendship."

"Oh thank goodness!" Lilymoon said, sounding relieved. Everypony turned to stare at her. She blushed and turned to Scootaloo. "I thought you were mad at me for some reason."

"No!" Scootaloo exclaimed. "You're awesome. Things have just been different lately." Scootaloo looked at Ambermoon.

"But I guess different isn't bad. It's just… different."

"No matter what else changes, you're always gonna be one of my best friends," Apple Bloom said. "And when you're in trouble, I'll be there. So next time my best friend says that she sees a scary, old pony coming after her, I promise I'm going to believe her."

"That's good," Sweetie Belle said with a shaky voice as the train pulled into the Ponyville train station. "Because as your other best friend, I want to tell you that there's a scary, old pony coming after us." She pointed out the window.

The Olden Pony was waiting for them at the train station.

"Thought you fillies could hide from me, did you?" The Olden Pony leered at them, pressing her face against the train window. Sweetie Belle leaped back from it so fast, she knocked over Scootaloo.

"No horseplay please," a passing conductor warned them. Scootaloo watched as he opened the carriage door and passengers exited the train, passing the Olden Pony without a glance.

"It's just like at the Wonderbolts show. Nopony sees her but us," whispered Lilymoon.

"But why? And where did she come from?" Ambermoon frowned.

"And how do we get rid of her?" Sweetie Belle wailed.

"That sounds like a job for the Cutie Mark Crusaders! I call an emergency meeting to order!" Apple Bloom blurted. Despite the spooky situation, Scootaloo had to hold back a laugh. Leave it to Apple Bloom to follow club procedure, even when they were being stalked by a ghost story come to life.

The last pony stepped out onto the train platform. Scootaloo hurled herself against the carriage door and slammed it shut, locking it before the Olden Pony could force her way onboard. Furious, the ancient mare scraped her single shoeless hoof against the glass of the window. It made a horrible grating sound.

"WHERE IS MY RUSTY HORSESHOE?" the Olden Pony groaned.

"Can we have this meeting somewhere else?" Scootaloo asked. The others were happy to agree, and they ran through the train car to the next one down the line.

"Everypony, think," Apple Bloom commanded. "Scootaloo, you were the first one of us to see the Olden Pony. Do you have any idea what you did to make her show up?" Scootaloo had been asking herself the same question ever since the slumber party. Unfortunately, she hadn't come up with any answers. She shook her head.

"You first saw her at our house, right?" Lilymoon asked. "So we should go back there and retrace your steps. Maybe that will give us a clue."

The train car shook with a heavy impact from its roof. The fillies froze and listened as heavy hoof-falls echoed above them. *CLANK CLANK CLANK THUMP! CLANK CLANK CLANK THUMP!* It was the sound of three horseshoes and one hoof. The Olden Pony was on top of the train. She was looking for a way in. And the emergency hatch was just over their heads.

"She can't chase us all if we split up," Scootaloo said. "Ambermoon, you run toward the front of the train. I'll go to the back." Ambermoon nodded.

"I'm coming with you," Apple Bloom told Scootaloo firmly.

"Me too!" Sweetie Belle squeaked.

"Guess that means we get some sister time," Lilymoon told Ambermoon. Scootaloo didn't think they seemed too happy about it. But there wasn't time to discuss that, because just then, the Olden Pony popped open the emergency door above them and squinted down, her red eye rolling in its socket.

"Did you miss me?" She brayed a terrifying laugh and lunged at the fillies.

"Meet us at our house!" Ambermoon yelled as she pushed open the train car door. She dashed off in the direction of the engine, Lilymoon hot on her hocks. Scootaloo, Apple Bloom, and Sweetie Belle jumped on the platform a moment later and raced in the other direction. The voice of the Olden Pony howled behind them:

"You can't run from me! I'll find you wherever you go!"

And that was the scariest thought of all.

CHAPTER TEN

The CMCs ran until they reached the bottom of Horseshoe Hill, where they stopped to gasp for breath. Scootaloo wished she had her scooter. No way a three-shoed pony could keep up with them then!

"Is she gone?" Sweetie Belle panted. The Crusaders looked around nervously, but it seemed they had finally lost the Olden Pony. Then Scootaloo had a troubling thought.

"I hope that doesn't mean she's chasing Ambermoon and Lilymoon instead," Scootaloo said.

Apple Bloom looked thoughtful. "When did you become such good friends with Ambermoon?" she asked.

Scootaloo shrugged. "I guess when she started being nice to me. She's actually kind of cool, once you spend time with her."

"Yeah…but do you think you can trust her?" Apple Bloom pressed.

"It *was* her candy cane that turned Twist into a werepony," Sweetie Belle pointed out.

"We don't know that's true." Apple Bloom frowned. Scootaloo started to worry that they were heading toward another disagreement. But then Apple Bloom's expression cleared. "I guess we just don't have all the facts yet. And it wouldn't be right to blame Ambermoon for anythin' until we know the whole story."

"Right," Scootaloo agreed with the tiniest sigh of relief.

Hoofbeats sounded behind them, and the trio spun, startled. But instead of the glare of a single red eye, they found

Lilymoon and Ambermoon.

"I'm *so glad* you're not the Olden Pony!" Sweetie Belle said.

"Um, thanks?" Lilymoon said. "Now, let's get to the house before she *does* show up."

The group climbed the hill to the forbidding home atop it.

"Did you ever think about getting a welcome mat?" Sweetie Belle suggested as they all stepped onto the rickety porch.

"No," Ambermoon and Lilymoon answered in unison.

Scootaloo led her friends inside to the giant staircase beyond the foyer. She pointed a hoof.

"There. That's where I first saw the Olden Pony," she told them.

"So we need to work backward from here," Ambermoon said. "Before you ran in this room, we were in the kitchen."

"Yeah." Scootaloo nodded. "I heard the Olden Pony in there. And before that, we walked across the yard…and before that, I was in the greenhouse, and before *that*—"

"Wait. What were you doing in the greenhouse?" Lilymoon asked with a frown. Scootaloo blushed. Now that she thought about it, admitting she was running away from Ambermoon did sound pretty silly.

"She got lost." Ambermoon smoothly covered for her new friend. "I found her in the greenhouse." Scootaloo shot her a grateful look, then picked up the tale.

"And before that, I was in the kitchen. Which is where I went after I left the sleepover."

"Every part of that story sounds pretty normal, except the greenhouse," Apple Bloom mused.

"I'm not sure anything here is normal," Sweetie Belle murmured, pointing a hoof. The other fillies followed it to see Blue Moon headed toward them, "walking" a pair of bats on tiny leashes.

"Hello, Father," Lilymoon and Ambermoon chorused.

"Hello, hello." Blue Moon grinned back. Scootaloo always felt like there was something off about that smile—it was as though you could count every one of Blue Moon's teeth. And some of them looked sharp. "Enjoy your visit with your friends! I'm off to walk Bram and Bela."

Every time she encountered the Moon sisters' odd parents, Scootaloo was glad she lived with Aunt Holiday and Auntie Lofty.

The fillies headed for the kitchen. But after opening drawers to find only cobwebs and peering into the refrigerator, which seemed to be housing some kind of mold experiment, they decided to move on to the greenhouse.

The air in the greenhouse was humid and heavy. Scootaloo almost felt as if she were swimming in a sea of plants.

"Show us where you went on the night of the slumber party," Apple Bloom prompted. Scootaloo tried to remember her exact path, but things looked very different in the daytime.

"I ran toward the back," she said, trotting deeper into the green glass enclosure. Her eye fell on a crooked ceramic pot. Now *that* she recognized. It matched the bruise on her forehead. "And I bumped into this!" She reached a hoof toward the soft feathery plant. Ambermoon quickly swatted it away.

"Don't touch that plant!" she said sharply. Scootaloo felt a knot form in her stomach. She already *had* touched it—two nights ago.

"Why?" she asked, hoping to sound breezy. "What would happen if I did?"

Ambermoon arched an eyebrow. "It's a fear fern," she explained.

Lilymoon nodded in recognition. "Oh yeah! I didn't know Dad was growing those."

"What do fear ferns do?" Sweetie Belle wondered. Scootaloo saw she was eyeing the plant as if it were a chimera ready to pounce.

"They give life to the thing that frightens you the most. But only you can see it," Ambermoon said grimly. "Sound familiar?"

"Okay, yes. I bumped into that plant and picked it up," Scootaloo admitted. "But I don't know why it made the Olden Pony show up. I'm totally over my fear of her! Mostly."

"That still doesn't explain why *we* can see the Olden Pony." Apple Bloom frowned. "We never touched the fern."

Ambermoon didn't have an answer for that.

"So now that we know what caused the problem, what's the cure?" Sweetie Belle wanted to know. Ambermoon and Lilymoon exchanged a worried look.

"There *isn't* one!" came a creaky voice from behind a cactus.

The fillies whipped their heads toward the voice. It was Auntie Eclipse. *When did she come in the greenhouse?* Scootaloo wondered. Had she just been hiding there all along?

"That is, there isn't a cure unless you know me." Auntie Eclipse chuckled uproariously. Scootaloo laughed, too, though she wasn't sure what was so funny. She was just glad to know that there was a way to get rid of the Olden Pony.

"Follow me. Let's have some tea and a nice chat," Auntie Eclipse said, making her way out of the greenhouse.

Lilymoon and Ambermoon followed their aunt, and after a moment, the Crusaders did, too.

Auntie Eclipse led the young ponies to the library. It smelled like dust and age and books. Light filtered down through grimy windows and cobwebbed shelves, casting eerie spotlights. Scootaloo knew that Auntie Eclipse usually didn't let visitors into this place. But today, the strange, old pony seemed downright social!

Auntie Eclipse patted some moth-eaten cushions and invited the fillies to sit. Apple Bloom plopped down on one, and a huge puff of dust exploded from it. She sneezed loudly. Scootaloo decided to just stand.

"Get the tea tray, would you, dear?" Auntie Eclipse asked Ambermoon.

"Are you sure that's a good ide—" Lilymoon began, but Auntie Eclipse turned a sour eye on her niece, and she fell silent.

Ambermoon returned with a tray of strange small sandwiches and what appeared to be raisin cookies. Scootaloo watched as Sweetie Belle politely took one, and then dropped it in shock as the "raisins" moved.

"On second thought, we're not very hungry," Sweetie Belle said.

So much for trying to be polite, Scootaloo thought.

Auntie Eclipse poured tea for everypony, but none of them took a sip. "It's so nice you young ponies came to visit me." Auntie Eclipse smiled. It seemed to Scootaloo that she'd forgotten why they were all there in the first place.

"We're hoping you can tell us more about the fear fern. Why did it affect all of us when only Scootaloo touched it? And can you give us the cure?" Ambermoon gently prompted her aunt.

"Your father has been breeding especially strong fear ferns. Normally, they only work on the pony who touches them. But Blue Moon's ferns are contagious. This little Pegasus," Auntie Eclipse said, shaking an admonishing hoof at Scootaloo, "infected everypony she touched with her fear spores."

Scootaloo gasped. Not only was the Olden Pony's appearance her fault…she'd spread the problem to her friends, too.

"You said there was a cure," Lilymoon reminded Auntie Eclipse.

"So I did, so I did." The old pony nodded. "Got it off a traveling salespony from Saddle Arabia many moons ago."

She rummaged around in a weathered cabinet and pulled out a vial of blue liquid. Auntie Eclipse held it up to her eye and shook the bottle. Then she nodded. "Should be just enough for you five in here." Scootaloo's heart sank.

"You five?" she asked weakly. Auntie Eclipse turned her sharp gaze on Scootaloo.

"Well, yes. How many ponies did you touch, dear?" Scootaloo started to count.

"Um, both of my aunts. And Pinkie Pie and the Cakes when we were looking for Rainbow Dash. And Rainbow Dash…"

"And Rarity. Miss Cheerilee. Big McIntosh. Featherweight…. All the ponies in line at the market when we squeezed past them—" Ambermoon added.

"Don't forget the ponies on the train," Apple Bloom chimed in.

"And all the ponies we passed in the stands at the Canterlot Wonderbolts show. And the announcer," Sweetie Belle said, her eyes getting huge.

"So…a lot," Lilymoon finished. Auntie Eclipse clucked her tongue.

"Oh dear. That's bad. You see, if enough ponies believe in the same fear…it becomes a permanent part of our world. The same way a strong friendship can create magic. In this case, a shared fright feeds strength to whatever is feared. Your Olden Pony just went from being a foal's ghost story to a real problem."

Scootaloo plopped down on a cushion in defeat, ignoring the dust that plumed up around her. She'd unleashed a terror on Ponyville. Maybe even on Canterlot. And there was no way to stop it.

CHAPTER TWELVE

"You really think Twilight can help us?" Scootaloo asked for the seventh time. Lilymoon, Ambermoon, and the Crusaders were racing toward Princess Twilight Sparkle's castle. Even though she'd said the same thing the last six times, Sweetie Belle reassured Scootaloo.

"Twilight's saved Equestria more times than I can count! Besides, our sisters and their friends are the bravest ponies we know!"

A screaming streak of rainbow zoomed past them. Scootaloo paused, frowning in confusion. Was that...?

"Rainbow Dash?" she called.

The colorful blur did a three-point turn in midair and blazed back toward them. It was Rainbow Dash, and she looked terrified.

"Did you see her? Is she here?" Rainbow Dash asked, glancing around jerkily.

"Who?" asked Apple Bloom.

"The Olden Pony! She's terrorizing the town!" Rainbow Dash was freaking out. Scootaloo hated to see her idol so upset. Especially since *she* was the one responsible for passing the fear fern spores to Rainbow Dash. "Go ahead. Say it. I was wrong; you were right. The Olden Pony is real! And she keeps screaming for her rusty horseshoe. Why would anypony want a rusty horseshoe? It doesn't make any sense!" Rainbow Dash gestured wildly.

"Don't worry. We're on our way to get Princess Twilight. We think she can fix this," Scootaloo told her.

"What? But Twilight's in town. Where the Olden Pony is! You don't want to go there!" Rainbow Dash tried to drag Scootaloo in the opposite direction.

"We have…a…plan!" Ambermoon said, grabbing Scootaloo and trying to pull her back.

"Now, what in the deep-dish strudel is goin' on here?" Applejack's voice rang out. As she walked up, Fluttershy at her side, she tipped her hat back to squint at the odd scene. "Are y'all playin' tug-of-war with Scootaloo?"

Apple Bloom took a deep breath and tried to explain everything as fast as she could. "Scootaloo bumped into a fear fern at Lilymoon's house and now the Olden Pony is real and everypony who Scootaloo touched can see her and—"

Applejack stomped a hoof to interrupt her little sister. "Now, Apple Bloom. You know I only want the truth."

"We'll show them, won't we?" came a terrifyingly familiar voice. Rainbow Dash and the fillies jumped, startled to see the Olden Pony creep out from behind a stand of trees.

"Where'd she come from?" Sweetie Belle whimpered.

"Where'd *who* come from?" Fluttershy asked, looking quizzically from the cowering ponies to Applejack.

"The Olden Pony," Scootaloo said weakly. The spooky old mare looked different now—somehow more solid. Bigger. And much scarier. Auntie Eclipse was right, Scootaloo realized. The ponies' fear was making her stronger. The Olden Pony advanced on the group, muttering horribly under her breath. Scootaloo shrank back.

Fluttershy looked at her in concern. "Oh no. It sounds like you're seeing things. Maybe you're getting sick. Do you have a fever?" Fluttershy laid a cool hoof on Scootaloo's forehead before she could jerk away.

"Don't touch her!" the Crusaders and Moon sisters yelled.

Fluttershy leaped back, startled and hurt. "Why not?"

"Because now you're mine, too," came a voice like the sound of creaking hinges.

Fluttershy's eyes grew wide and she backed away, trembling. *"It's the…the… Olden Pony!"*

Applejack frowned at Fluttershy, then

her expression cleared with a realization.

"Oh, I get it. This is one of your practical jokes, huh, Dash? Okay, I'll play. *Ooooh.* I'm so scared of the Golden Pony." Applejack pretended to be frightened.

"*Olden* Pony!" Rainbow Dash corrected her.

"Fine. Now. Aren't we supposed to be havin' a little chitchat with these fillies about their behavior at your Wonderbolts show?" Applejack asked. Neither Rainbow Dash nor Fluttershy answered. Their eyes were locked on the red Cyclops-like glare of the ancient mare. Applejack sighed. "Guess it's up to me, then. C'mon, y'all," she told the CMCs and their friends, shooing them forward with a hoof, "let's go." And then Applejack nudged Scootaloo.

Scootaloo watched miserably as Applejack finally saw what the others were reacting to. Her jaw dropped, and her eyes grew wide in terror. She backed up, next to Rainbow Dash and Fluttershy, quaking. Then all three of them stampeded away, the Olden Pony cackling in terrible pursuit.

"Listen," Ambermoon told the others, "remember what Auntie Eclipse said? Shared fear gives the Olden Pony more power. Maybe she'll go away if we can convince everypony in town not to be afraid."

"First we have to convince ourselves," Apple Bloom pointed out.

CHAPTER THIRTEEN

When the group of five fillies arrived in town and turned down Ponyville's main street in search of Twilight, Scootaloo knew that there was no chance of doing what Ambermoon had suggested.

The town was in chaos. Ponies screamed and ran in terror. The Olden Pony almost seemed to be everywhere! Scootaloo watched as the Olden Pony popped out of an apple cart to scare Big McIntosh. As he stampeded off, the spooky pony disappeared, only to reappear in an alleyway, startling Miss Cheerilee. She even chased Filthy Rich in circles around the town square.

"I'll give you as many bits as you

want," Filthy Rich whimpered, "just leave me alone!"

"I don't want bits. *I want my rusty horseshoe!"* the Olden Pony proclaimed. Filthy Rich leaped into an open pickle barrel and pulled the lid on top, trying to hide. But the Olden Pony just cackled and gave the barrel a shove, sending it (and Filthy Rich) rolling down the street. Ponies leaped out of the way of the sloshing, screaming barrel. The Crusaders, Lilymoon, and Ambermoon ducked behind a building to get away from the hysteria.

"Scootaloo. You never finished your story," Lilymoon said suddenly.

Scootaloo was confused. "What story?"

"The Olden Pony story. How does it end? What makes her go away?"

Scootaloo shrugged. "The story doesn't

really have an end," she said, shaking her head. "She's just always wandering Equestria, yelling for her rusty horseshoe."

"Why's she so upset, anyhow?" Apple Bloom wondered.

"Maybe she's lonely," Ambermoon said. The other ponies all turned to look at her. Ambermoon carefully didn't meet their eyes. "I mean...it's easy to be angry when you don't have any friends. Or you feel like nopony is listening to you." Scootaloo could tell Ambermoon was speaking from experience. She knew how that felt, too.

"Yeah, when you guys didn't believe me, and I thought I was losing you as friends, it was pretty much the worst feeling ever," Scootaloo admitted.

"You think that's how the Olden Pony

feels?" Sweetie Belle asked with wide eyes. "She just wants a friend?"

Scootaloo started to laugh at the very idea of it, but then she paused. Why not? Nopony ever actually talked to the Olden Pony. They just ran away from her. That did sound pretty lonely.

"I think I might have an idea of how to stop everypony from being afraid," said Scootaloo. "But I'm gonna need some help."

"What are friends for?" Apple Bloom grinned. "We're in!"

Everypony seems to be talking at once, Scootaloo thought. Twilight and her friends sat at their thrones around the map table in the Castle of Friendship, arguing and recounting their horrific experiences with the Olden Pony. Lilymoon, Ambermoon, and the Crusaders stood nearby, waiting to get a word in edgewise. Finally, Twilight Sparkle raised her hooves to interrupt the cacophony.

"And the reason this ghost story became real is because your father is growing especially powerful fear ferns?" Twilight asked, fixing her eyes on Ambermoon and Lilymoon. Scootaloo squirmed for them. She'd been in trouble enough times to know how intense Twilight's gaze could be. "First the bogle, then the werepony, now this. I'm not sure I like how much dangerous magic seems to be coming from your family's house." Twilight frowned.

"It wasn't our father's plant. He's just… watching it for a friend," Lilymoon said quickly. Scootaloo blinked. Lilymoon was lying! It was just a small lie…but why? The other Crusaders glanced at Scootaloo. They'd noticed, too.

"Whatever the case, we need to stop this fear before it gets any stronger," Twilight said. She thought for a moment. "The Olden Pony keeps asking for her rusty horseshoe. Maybe we could try just giving her what she wants?" she suggested.

"I already tried that. It didn't work; she just knocked it aside and kept chasing us,"

Scootaloo explained. "But…I think I may have another idea." Twilight nodded for Scootaloo to continue. She felt a little nervous, laying out her plan to the bravest ponies in Equestria, but she cleared her throat and went for it. "We'll need everypony in town to help. Hopefully, that'll be enough to cover the ones I accidentally touched in Canterlot, too." Scootaloo looked around the room as she explained. "Spooky things aren't as scary when you understand them. And I think the Olden Pony just needs understanding and friendship." The others looked at her, waiting for her to go on. "So I thought we could all welcome her as our new friend," Scootaloo finished lamely.

"That's it? *That's* your plan?" Rainbow Dash asked in disbelief.

"It does seem rather simplistic," Rarity chimed in. And suddenly, all the ponies were talking over one another again.

"*Hey!*" Sweetie Belle yelled. The older ponies fell silent. Scootaloo was just as shocked as they were. She hadn't known such a loud noise could come out of Sweetie Belle. "You didn't believe us when we tried to tell you about the Timberwolf, either. Well, this time, you'd better listen! Or we'll all be in even worse trouble! I mean…uh…please," Sweetie Belle added politely.

"Sweetie Belle has a point," Twilight said dryly. "We did promise to listen to you fillies in the future. And I agree that friendship is stronger than fear. What do you need from us, Scootaloo?"

The tiniest hoofshaving of moon hung in the sky above the Ponyville town square. Scootaloo stood alone in the eerie darkness, shivering. She was beginning to rethink her plan. But it was a little late for that. She stepped bravely forward and yelled into the night.

"OLDEN PONY! I WANT TO TALK TO YOU!"

A freezing wind, colder than Scootaloo had ever felt, blew past. Icicles formed on the nearby eaves, and a chill danced down Scootaloo's back.

"Whoooo calls?" The Olden Pony's voice creaked, echoing from all corners of the town. The shadows cast by the shops

seemed to grow and mass together before revealing a huge figure with a single glowing flame of an eye. Scootaloo gulped. Fear had definitely made the ancient mare stronger. She tried to keep her voice steady as she answered.

"I do. Scootaloo. I hear you're looking for something."

"MY RUSTY HORSESHOE! WHERE IS IT? WHERRRRRRREEEE?" In the blink of an eye, the Olden Pony was towering over Scootaloo, her dark shawl seeming to blot out even the light of the stars.

"I already gave you one of those and you didn't want it," Scootaloo said, bravely holding her ground. "I think you're really looking for something else."

"WHAT?" the Olden Pony demanded, leering at Scootaloo.

"Friendship," Scootaloo said, forcing a smile despite her fear.

The Olden Pony hesitated. She seemed to be considering that. Scootaloo quickly continued, pressing her advantage. "I think nopony ever listens to you, so I will. That's what it means to be a friend. Tell me about your rusty horseshoe. Why do you want it so badly?"

The Olden Pony appeared confused. Scootaloo realized that this must be the first time the ancient mare hadn't had a pony run away from her. Maybe she wasn't sure what to do.

"I...*need it?*" the Olden Pony said, hesitantly raising the hoof without a shoe.

"Why does it have to be rusty?" Scootaloo asked. Her constant questions seemed to be keeping the Olden Pony from pouncing on her. Plus, she *had* always wondered about that.

"I'm not sure." The Olden Pony seemed to consider this, surprised.

"Then why don't you let your new friends give you something nicer?" Scootaloo suggested. She flared her wings wide and yelled, *"Now!"*

The doors of every building in the town square suddenly swung open, and the residents of Ponyville poured out. Scootaloo could see they looked nervous, but her friends led them forward. Everypony held something in their forehoof—each object the same yet different. The Olden Pony looked at them, then glared.

"WHERE'S MY RUSSSSSSTY HORSESHOOOOOEEEE?" she rasped menacingly.

"Try this on instead," Apple Bloom said, moving to stand alongside Scootaloo. She held out a candy-apple-red horseshoe for the Olden Pony. The ancient mare frowned and leaned down to examine it. "I painted it special for you, my new friend!"

"You can have this one, too," Sweetie Belle squeaked, joining Scootaloo's other side and trying not to tremble as she held out a soft embroidered horseshoe. "My sister helped me design it for you."

"And these are from us," Ambermoon said. She and Lilymoon held out horseshoes that were perfect opposites, like the sisters themselves. One shoe was white with a black stripe; the other was black with a white stripe.

"I…I…don't understand," the Olden Pony said, sounding unsure for the first time. *"You should be running from me!"*

"We don't run from our friends, silly!" Rainbow Dash said, flying up with a Wonderbolt-blue horseshoe in her hooves. It even had tiny lightning bolts decorating it, Scootaloo noticed.

One by one, the other ponies stepped forward to present their gifts to the surprised Olden Pony. Soon horseshoes of every shape, size, color, and material formed a pile in front of the ancient mare. Shiny shoes, polka-dot shoes, ribbon-wound shoes, flowery shoes, shoes that made music when you stepped on them. Cranky Doodle's shoe was made of an old toupee. And Pinkie Pie had baked a cupcake in the shape of a horseshoe.

"For when you get hungry on a walk," she explained brightly.

The Olden Pony just stood there, staring at the mountain of horseshoes. She looked around at the sea of smiling pony faces surrounding her.

"You're…not afraid?" the Olden Pony asked.

And then Scootaloo knew what she had to do. She didn't like it. But she was the only pony who could do it.

"Nope. We're just glad you're our friend," she said. And then she leaned close to the terrifying mare and hugged her. The Olden Pony froze…then patted Scootaloo's back with her unshod hoof.

"Well. Thank you, dearie," the Olden Pony said. And then…she disappeared, along with the pile of horseshoes.

The town square erupted in cheers!

"Yaaaay, Scootaloo! You did it! She's

gone! We're saved!" Ponies surrounded Scootaloo and hoisted her onto their shoulders. Scootaloo grinned, although she couldn't help but feel a little pang of guilt—after all, if she hadn't infected the ponies with the fear fern in the first place, none of this would've happened. Apple Bloom seemed to guess what she was thinking, and she beamed up at her friend.

"Just go with it!" she said.

The next morning, everypony worked together to clean up the chaos in the town from the terror of the day before. By noon, it was as though the Olden Pony had never been there.

"That's the power of friendship in action," Applejack said, admiring the sparkling town square. *And good soap*, Scootaloo thought, smiling to herself.

The Crusaders, Lilymoon, and Ambermoon joined Twilight and her friends at Sugarcube Corner for a well-deserved treat after their cleaning spree. Pinkie Pie trotted out with more of the horseshoe cupcakes she had baked, but the fillies declined to try them.

"Uh…too soon," Scootaloo explained to Pinkie.

"More for me!" Pinkie Pie shrugged and happily nommed the cakes herself.

"Hey…" Rainbow Dash pulled Scootaloo aside with a wing. "I just wanted to say I'm sorry for giving you a hard time about the Olden Pony. Just 'cause I didn't see her doesn't mean I shouldn't have listened to you. We okay?"

"Totally," Scootaloo said, relieved that things were right with Rainbow Dash again.

"And before I forget, these are for you," Rainbow Dash said, holding out five tickets with the Wonderbolts logo on them. "VIP tickets for you and your friends to our Cloudsdale Expo. It's about twenty percent cooler than the Flyfest," she added with a wink.

"Really?" Scootaloo couldn't believe it. "You sure you want us there after last time?"

"Just try not to shut down *this* show." Rainbow Dash smiled, giving Scootaloo's head a playful noogie.

As the other ponies finished up their treats, Twilight Sparkle addressed the group.

"There have been a lot of strange things happening in Ponyville lately. And while we've managed to handle all of them before they got too out of hoof, I'm worried about what will come next." Twilight turned to the Unicorn sisters. "Lilymoon, Ambermoon. I think it's time my friends and I had a talk with your family. I have quite a few questions about the safety of the magic they're practicing."

Lilymoon and Ambermoon shared a worried look.

"Our family is pretty private," Lilymoon said at the same time as Ambermoon spoke: "I don't think that's such a good idea." Scootaloo was pretty sure it was the first time she'd seen the sisters agree on something. They must have really not wanted Twilight to visit the house on Horseshoe Hill. But Twilight persisted.

"I know it might be an uncomfortable conversation," Twilight said. "But it's necessary. I don't want any more dangerous surprises in our town. Now, if you'll please lead us to your parents?"

Lilymoon and Ambermoon hung their heads. But they nodded and started out of Sugarcube Corner, Twilight and her friends following.

"I hope we didn't get them into trouble," Sweetie Belle worried when they were gone. Scootaloo nodded. The Moon family wasn't the most understanding bunch of ponies.

"Especially since we just made friends with Ambermoon," Apple Bloom added. "You were right, Scootaloo. She's nice!"

"And brave," Sweetie Belle agreed.

"Yeah, both sisters are," Scootaloo said. But something was still bothering her. "Do you think we can trust them? I mean, I can't imagine either of them wanting to turn anypony into a Timberwolf."

"But if they didn't…then who did?" Apple Bloom wondered.

"And why did Lilymoon lie to Twilight about the fear fern?" Sweetie Belle asked.

None of them had any answers. And Scootaloo was sure that if they didn't find out what was going on soon, life in Ponyville would get even weirder *and* more dangerous. She looked at her two best friends and smiled. No matter what mysteries were hiding on Horseshoe Hill, she knew that as long as she had the two of them by her side, the Cutie Mark Crusaders could handle *any*thing that came their way. At least…she hoped so.

The Pony was intrigued. As annoying as those Cutie Mark Crusaders were, this time, they had actually been helpful. The Pony hadn't realized a fear fern could be so powerful. It would work nicely with The Pony's plan. The Princess of Friendship may be sticking her muzzle where it didn't belong, but soon it would be too late for her to do anything. Things were starting to fall into place. The Pony would enter the Livewood. And then, the real fun would start.

Penumbra Quill grew up in Califoalnia and started her career as a travel writer, journeying across Equestria to report on the hottest vacation trends. A visit to Las Pegasus changed everything when Penumbra discovered a ghost in the city's spectacular new resort, The Whinny. That trip changed Penumbra's life forever. Since then, she has dedicated herself to writing true tales of Equestria's spooky and supernatural happenings to chill and thrill her readers. She currently resides just outside Ponyville with her pet Phoenix, Firebrand, and enjoys catching Wonderbolts shows whenever she can.

Enjoy
Spooktacular Fun!
Now on DVD!

PONY TRICK OR TREAT

My Little Pony
FRIENDSHIP is MAGIC